Ans	_____	M.L.	_____
ASH	_____	MLW	_____
Bev	_____	Mt.Pl	_____
C.C.	_____	NLM	_____
C.P.	_____	Ott	_____
Dick	03/10	PC	_____
DRZ	_____	PH	_____
ECH	_____	P.P.	8/07
ECS	_____	Pion.P.	_____
Gar	_____	Q.A.	_____
GRM	_____	Riv	_____
GSP	_____	RPP	_____
G.V.	_____	Ross	_____
Har	_____	S.C.	11/07
JPCP	_____	St.A.	_____
KEN	_____	St.J	_____
K.L.	_____	St.Joa	6/08
K.M.	_____	St.M.	_____
L.H.	_____	Sgt	_____
LO	_____	T.H.	_____
Lyn	_____	TLLO	_____
L.V.	_____	T.M.	_____
McC	_____	T.T.	12/06
McG	_____	Ven	_____
McQ	6/08	Vets	_____
MIL	_____	VP	_____
	Heiland (06/07)	Wat	_____
	_____	Wed	_____
	_____	WIL	3/07
	_____	W.L.	_____

THE CINDERELLA
FACTOR

THE CINDERELLA FACTOR

BY

SOPHIE WESTON

First published in Great Britain 2006
Large Print edition 2006
Harlequin Mills & Boon Limited,
Eton House, 18-24 Paradise Road,
Richmond, Surrey TW9 1SR

© Sophie Weston 2006

ISBN-13: 978 0 263 19003 8
ISBN-10:   0 263 19003 X

Set in Times Roman 16½ on 17¾ pt.
16-0906-56870

Printed and bound in Great Britain
by Antony Rowe Ltd, Chippenham, Wiltshire

PROLOGUE

THREE continents watched foreign correspondent Patrick Burns torpedo his brilliant career on live television.

The first person to notice was the assistant editor in the London office.

'Oh, no,' she said. 'He's going to take sides.'

Nonsense, they said. Patrick Burns had just been voted International Reporter of the Year. When he was on a roll like that, why on earth would he risk his job?

'For the second time,' muttered Ed Lassells, the head honcho, though nobody noticed.

Besides, Patrick always said it himself, when he lectured at conferences or made one of his modest, witty speeches accepting yet another award. 'We can't get involved,' he would say. 'We're journalists. We're impartial or we're nothing.'

But that had been before Patrick had lain on his face in the dust for twenty minutes while snipers held their fire for the sake of the eleven-year-old village boy squatting beside him. Patrick was involved now, come hell or high water.

His cameraman had suspected something was up the night he finally broke loose. A great moon gave them a wavering train of dark shadow across the stony mountainside. It picked out anything shiny: the face of Patrick's watch, the screen of a cellular phone, a metal button. They didn't need a torch to guide their scramble up the bleak slope.

'Blasted moon. We might as well be in a spotlight,' muttered Tim, stopping for a moment, a hand to his side. The air was thin at that height, and he was not as used to it as Patrick. Or as fit.

'Then let's hope the enemy is looking the other way,' said Patrick, still climbing.

'The girls in the office should see you now,' Tim said dryly.

Patrick did not falter, but he gave a bark of laughter. 'You mean the pin-up portrait in the velvet jacket?'

Tim was surprised. 'You know about it?'

Patrick looked over his shoulder. 'The poster of me in the girls' restroom looking like a Las Vegas gambler? Sure, I know about it. Last Christmas party they asked me in there to sign it.'

Tim was even more surprised. The girls shivered in mock trepidation whenever Patrick's name was mentioned. But, then again, they laid elaborate plans to get him on a date.

It was an office game. Only one girl had ever gone out with him seriously. It had taken her three weeks to come to her senses. Then, when Patrick had gone off abroad on his next assignment, she'd confided to her best friend, the Balkan specialist—and thence to the whole company—that Patrick was tricky.

'Very tricky,' nice Corinna had said, shaken out of her light-hearted sophistication. 'If you let him take you to bed, it's like he doesn't forgive you.'

'Doesn't like loose women?' the Balkan specialist had asked, fascinated by this anachronism.

But Corinna had shaken her head, sobered by her brush with blazing Patrick Burns. 'It's like it makes him hate himself.'

Which, of course, had been much too intriguing to keep to themselves.

There was much speculation on Patrick Burns's inner demons in the ladies' cloakroom. A more sober picture of him from an awards ceremony, frowning and intense in an impeccable dinner jacket, appeared on the wall of the newsroom beneath the international time clocks. Lisa, the receptionist, dubbed him Count Dracula, and most of the women in the place agreed—and sighed. Much to the annoyance of their male colleagues.

'The man's a sex god,' the Balkan specialist had said in a matter-of-fact voice when her boss had wondered aloud, irritably, what Patrick Burns had got that other men didn't have. 'Get over it.'

'But you say yourselves that he isn't kind to his women,' roly-poly Donald had said, bewildered. 'I mean, that's not the modern woman's dream man, is it?'

The Balkan specialist had grinned. 'Who needs dreams? Patrick can give you one hell of a sexy nightmare.'

Now Tim bit back a smile. He was very keen on the Balkan specialist. If she saw Patrick Burns now, she wouldn't think he was sexy, Tim thought with faintly guilty satisfaction.

Like Tim himself, Patrick was swathed in a triple-lined all-weather jacket. The hood had a fur inset and his gloves would have got him up Everest without frostbite. It was the right gear for this bitter mountainside. But suave Count Dracula was definitely out.

Patrick put down the equipment he was

carrying and shaded his eyes, looking across the valley. The distant peaks were like a silhouette out of a Victorian *Arabian Nights*. But he was not looking at the mountains. He was looking at the town in the plain. From their vantage point, it looked incredibly small. Clouds of smoke, colourless in the night air, were billowing up from the road they had travelled with the tiny group of stunned, silent refugees only this morning. The village where the refugees had stopped, hoping for a brief rest, was now invisible behind the smokescreen. The thud of bombs reached them a few seconds later.

'Poor bastards,' said Tim, following Patrick's gaze.

A muscle worked in Patrick's jaw. He had not shaved for two days now, and the throbbing muscle was very clear under the residual beard.

But all he said was, 'Yes.'

Tim made the satellite link and went through the routine methodically. He had done it three times a day for the last ten days, and he and his opposite number in London had it down to a fine art now. They finished with plenty of time to spare, and Tim stood down, idling, waiting for the countdown to air time.

Patrick stood where Tim told him to. He had

to push the fur-lined hood of his parka back to insert his own earpiece.

'You look like a brigand,' said Tim.

The brown fur at Patrick's shoulders was ruffled in the icy breeze, brindling his uncropped dark hair. Between the gypsy hair and two days' growth of beard, Patrick did not look so different from some of the hard-eyed men they had met on commandeered tanks in the field.

Patrick gave a grim smile. 'Thank you.'

Suddenly, Tim's vague unease crystallised. Everything began to make sense—the long hair, the beard, the urgent conversations with the interpreter. Even giving away his rations like that to the bedraggled locals. It was as if Patrick was wound so tightly he no longer needed food. As if he was preparing for a great adventure…

'You're going underground, aren't you?' Tim said slowly.

Patrick nodded. 'I'll give it a try, anyway.'

'Man, you're crazy,' said Tim, awed.

The countdown to live broadcast started.

Against the black sky, lights flared intermittently. The distant *wump, wump* of bombs landing drifted across to them. It was out of synch with the flares.

In their earpieces, they could hear the newscaster setting the scene. The man's voice said in their ears, '…and, in the mountains, our correspondent Patrick Burns. Any sign of the struggle abating, Patrick?'

Over him, the editor said, 'Three, two, one—cue Patrick.'

Patrick launched fluently into broadcaster mode. Only it wasn't the agreed script at all.

He said, 'This is a terrible place.'

'What?' screamed the editor. 'Patrick, get back to the agreed line, you bastard.'

Patrick ignored the voice in his ear.

'The night air is bitterly cold, even worse than the day.' He was serene, intense. 'There has been a drought here for two years. The dust is everywhere. It's in our shoes, our clothes, the food in our packs. My cameraman and I have to keep scarves across our mouths or the dust gets in our throats.'

'The battle,' yelled the London editor. 'Talk about the battle, you insubordinate son of a camel.'

And for a moment Patrick did, listing the advances, the losses, the claims by both sides. He nodded to Tim and the camera swung slowly round to focus on him.

Oh, yes, he looked good on camera, Tim thought. Alert and reliable, like the captain of a ship. The sort of man you could trust. The public of the English-speaking world certainly trusted him. According to the company's latest annual report, he was Mercury News International's greatest asset.

It had to be that trick he had of looking straight into the camera, earnestly, as if he really *wanted* you to understand. He was doing it now. And he had finished with the battle.

'The bombs our government sold one side,' Patrick told the world, in his measured, unemotional way, 'hit the arms dumps our government sold the other. You can see the explosions in the night sky behind me.'

He gestured. Obediently, Tim ran a long, slow tracking shot along the smoky line of bomb fog. It went on, and on, and on.

'And while the bombardment goes on,' said Patrick levelly, as the camera tracked relentlessly, 'we come across little groups of people on the road. They have lost their homes. There is no food. There will not be any food next year, either.'

The editor was now keeping up a steady stream of profanity in their earpieces. Patrick talked through it as if he could not hear the woman.

'This land had already been turned to concrete by drought. Now it is a junkyard of weapons.' He paused. 'Weapons made in the developed world. Sold by Western governments. Like ours.'

Tim brought the camera back to him. Patrick was shaking now. That had to be the fierce cold on his unprotected head. He did not seem to notice.

'There are mines here. And the rest. Nobody knows what is live and what is safe. Nobody *will* know until a farmer sets one off when he comes out to plant next year's crops. Or a child throws a ball and the earth explodes in his face.'

He was mesmerising, thought Tim, shaken in spite of his professional cynicism.

'And the truly terrible thing,' Patrick told the camera quietly, 'is that nobody knows how to stop it. Too many people are making money out of it.'

The furore in their earpieces quietened. A new voice spoke. An authoritative voice.

'Patrick, stop this,' it said coldly. 'Give me the balance of power analysis.'

Veteran newsman Ed Lassells ran a tight ship. You obeyed him or you walked.

Patrick went on as if he had not heard Ed Lassells, either. He was shaking with cold. 'For the last day my cameraman and I have been travelling with eight people from a village that doesn't exist any more.'

'Give me the analysis, Patrick,' said Ed, in a voice like lead.

Patrick ignored him so completely that Tim wondered if he had actually removed his earpiece. He realised suddenly that Patrick was not shaking with cold. It was passion.

It was unprofessional. By God, it was awesome.

'The adults are stunned,' Patrick told the camera levelly. 'They are being led by a boy of eleven. "Why?" I asked one of the women. "Because he is so young he does not yet know it is hopeless," she said.'

Even Tim, who had been there when the tired woman had said it, was moved.

'That boy saved my life,' said Patrick Burns starkly.

'Right, that's it. I'm pulling the plug,' said Ed.

They heard the studio presenter say, 'We seem to have lost contact with Patrick Burns. We'll try to link up again and bring you the rest of his dispatch later in the programme.'

Patrick said nothing. He drew a long breath, as if he had come to the end of a race that had pushed him to the limit. Then he pulled up the hood of his parka again and began to dismantle his microphone, quite as if nothing had happened. He looked very peaceful.

Through the earpiece Ed Lassells spoke again. Old, weary, infinitely cold. 'Well done, Patrick. That was professional suicide.'

Patrick said lightly, 'Hey, sometimes the truth is bigger than the sponsors.'

Ed didn't even bother to answer. The line went dead.

'Oh, boy, you are *so* out of a job,' said Tim, torn between sympathy and straightforward hero-worship. 'What are you going to do now?'

And Patrick Burns, prizewinner and danger addict, said, as if it were a joke, 'Justify my existence.'

CHAPTER ONE

JO ALMOND had finally worked out that she was not lovable when she was just fourteen.

It had hurt. But, after the first searing shock, Jo was philosophical about it. She'd known she had other things going for her. She was practical. She had found she could be brave. She didn't give up easily. She was energetic, clear-headed and calm. But lovable? Nah.

The man who finally taught her this painful lesson was her language teacher—a French student on teaching practice. He'd been twenty-three, with kind eyes and a passion for learning. For a while he'd believed in her. He'd been the only person in the whole world who had.

He'd also listened to her. Not for long, of course. But for a precious few hours she'd seen what it could be like if someone was on your side.

She ran away again. That time she'd got as far as Dover. She'd been just about to step on a ferry when a kindly policeman had caught up with her and organised her return home. Well, to her aunt's house. Jo would not call it home.

Jacques Sauveterre asked her to stay behind after French on her first afternoon back in school. By that time, Jo was good at keeping her own counsel. She stood there, not meeting his eyes, fidgeting.

'But why, Joanne? I would really like to understand this.'

'I wanted to go to France,' muttered Jo.

'But of course.'

She did look up at that. 'What?'

His kind eyes were twinkling. 'Everyone in their right mind wants to go to France. France is paradise. It is only natural. But maybe it would be easier if you waited until the school holidays?'

For a moment she stared at him, disbelieving. He wasn't shouting. He didn't think she was next stop to a criminal. He was laughing at her, but very gently.

She gave a tiny, cautious smile—just in case this was real.

He sat on the corner of the teacher's desk and looked at her gravely. 'You know, people keep telling me that you are a tear-away. You don't care about school. You hardly ever do your homework. But you don't seem like that in my class, Joanne.'

No one had looked at her like that before. So interested. So warm.

'Oh.'

'Now, why don't you tell me why you really ran away from home, hmm? The real reason?'

Well, that was impossible, of course. What could she say? *My so-called aunt hates me and her husband is a drunk who hits me?* No, she couldn't say that. Carol and Brian Grey were pillars of the community, and Jo had just demonstrated how irresponsible she was. No one would believe her if she said that.

But she told him a tiny bit of the truth. 'My aunt won't let me do Latin.'

He was utterly taken aback.

'Latin?'

'I asked if I could. She said no.'

Just as she said no to anything that Jo might enjoy or that might make her feel normal. It was not that Jo refused to do homework. Her aunt insisted that she do housework every night. And she had to make little Mark's tea and wash and mend his clothes. Jo didn't mind that. She loved Mark, who was the closest she had to a brother, in the same boat as she was and who loved her back. They took good care that the Greys didn't find out, though, and always growled at each other when Brian or Carol was around. If she knew they were close, Carol would find a way to use it against them. As she used everything else; even Jo's love of cars.

When Jacques Sauveterre called to protest about the block on Jo taking his extra new class in Latin, Carol was all concerned interest.

'Jo is a natural linguist, Mrs. Grey,' he told Carol earnestly in his melting French accent. 'It's a crime to keep her out of Latin.'

Carol widened her pansy brown eyes. 'But of course, Jo must do whatever she wants at school. She told us she *wanted* to do car maintenance classes.' She gave that tinkling, treacherous laugh and added, 'I suppose poor Geoff Rawlings isn't the pin-up he was, now that *you've* arrived.'

She didn't have to say it. The message was loud and clear. *Clumsy, plain teenage Jo has got a crush on you.* And, as so often with Carol, there was just a hint of truth among the lies. Jo *was* good with cars. She *did* like them. And everyone knew it.

It was Jacques's first job. The whole staffroom was warning him about the risk of teenage emotionalism. Carol Grey was pretty and appealing—and she sounded so sensible. He believed her. Of course he believed her.

Standing there listening, Jo was helpless. She burned with shame.

'Maybe it's adolescence,' Carol Grey told him sadly, glancing at Jo with spurious kindness. 'She's such a great gangling thing, poor child, and with those shoulders. Like a wardrobe. I suppose a man can't really understand that, Monsieur Sauveterre.'

Jacques blushed. In the face of this gentle female mockery he forgot all his campaigning zeal and nodded.

'Oh,' he said, avoiding Jo's eyes. 'Well, I'm sure you know best, Mrs Grey.'

And he fled. Leaving her to deal with the fallout on her own.

Carol's mask dropped frighteningly the moment the door closed behind him. 'So you thought you'd run away with the pretty little Frog Prince, did you?' Carol said softly. 'Think again. Who would want a giraffe like you?'

Jo put her head down and didn't answer.

It maddened Carol. 'If you've got time to do bloody Latin, you've got time to help me in the business. You can start filing tonight.'

So there was the end of ever doing home-work again.

'No point in getting ideas above your station,' Carol said, again and again. 'The next thing we'd know, you'd be wanting to go to college or some-thing.' And she laughed heartily. 'Much better if you stay here and learn to do as you're told. That's all you're good for. All you'll ever be good for.'

Jacques Sauveterre did not talk to Jo after that. Never singled her out in class again. Never so much as smiled at her when she took Mark to the under-elevens football game that he coached. He was kind to Mark, though. Jo tried to be grateful for that.

And his example also inspired someone else. The car maintenance teacher was more street-wise than Jacques Sauveterre.

'She just doesn't fit in,' he said to Carol. 'The others are tough kids in combats. Jo isn't. But she soon will be if you aren't careful.'

That night, every garment disappeared from Jo's wardrobe except two pairs of army surplus trousers and some khaki tee-shirts.

'See if Monsieur le Frog looks at you now,' said Carol, gleeful.

'I'm sorry, Jo,' said Mr Rawlings. 'Hope I

didn't make things worse. Well, at least I can give you the history of the combustion engine.'

He started lending her books on classic cars. Jo read them at school in the breaks. She also became a first-class mechanic.

Carol never knew. She thought she was keeping Jo fully occupied, caring for Mark and working in her home sales business. It gave her a whipping boy and she enjoyed that. She even laughed when Brian Grey came home drunk and hit out at Jo.

'Life isn't all pretty Frenchmen, kid. Get over it.'

On her sixteenth birthday Jo ran away for the fourth and final time.

Oh, the Greys looked for her. They were being paid good money for her keep. Anyway, Carol didn't like her victims to get away. It spoiled her fun for weeks.

But this time, Jo had planned well. She knew where her papers were because Carol had taken delight in showing her the betraying birth certificate.

'There you are. "Father unknown". You're a little illegit. Nobody wanted you. They paid us to take you off their hands.'

Jo had looked at it stonily. The one thing she

would not do, *ever*, was cry. It drove Carol wild with frustration.

So she'd just taken note of where Carol had put it away. And that night she took it, along with her passport and an oddly shaped envelope she had never seen before. But it was addressed to her, in unfamiliar handwriting.

Inside there was an old book—a hardback with cheap card covers. It had pen and ink drawings on the printed pages and smelled of old-fashioned nursery sweets—liquorice and barley sugar and mint humbugs. It was called *The Furry Purry Tiger*. It was a present for a child.

Maybe someone had wanted her after all, thought Jo. For a while, anyway.

She didn't get too excited about it. She had enough to do just surviving in the next three years. And making sure that Mark did not have to pay for her defection.

She went on the road—moving from place to place, doing casual jobs, finding new places to stay every few weeks. One way or another, though, she always managed to call Mark once a week. They got adept at making contact without Carol finding out. They always ended by saying, 'See you soon.'

When she ended a call Jo always thought: I'll

get Mark away. I *will*. And then we'll go to France, which is earthly paradise, and be happy.

Another thing she'd managed to do was keep in touch with Monsieur Sauveterre. Whether he'd seen the marks Brian's fists left or whether he was just kind-hearted, she never knew. Maybe it was because he coached Mark's football club and it was nothing to do with Jo at all. But before he'd gone home, he'd pressed his address in France into her hand.

'You and Mark. When you come to France, you must look me up. You will always be welcome. I promise you.'

For Jo, it was like insurance. Every so often, when she was settled somewhere for a few months, she sent him a postcard with her address. It was a way of saying, *Remember your promise*.

Jacques always replied. He'd even invited them to his wedding.

And then one day, when she spoke to Mark, she knew they could not put it off any longer. He was still only fifteen, but that couldn't be helped. One Saturday morning, on a borrowed cell-phone, Mark's voice sounded odd. More than odd. Old. Very, very tired. Or ill.

At once Jo knew what had happened. Drunken

Brian Grey had beaten him. Badly this time. Just as he had once beaten Jo.

Only once. The second time he'd tried, the night before her birthday, Jo had got him in an arm lock, ground his telephone under her heel and locked him in the cupboard under the stairs. That had been the evening she'd taken her papers and the money she had saved, from the babysitting that Brian and Carol did not know about, and melted into the night.

Now, she knew, Mark would have to do the same.

'Get out of there *now*,' she said, ice cool now that the worst had happened. 'Do you know where he keeps your birth certificate and your passport?'

'Yes. I saw him put them in the old biscuit barrel the last time he changed the hiding place.'

It figured. As well as being violent, Brian Grey was sly and secretive. But nobody ever said he was bright. What an uncle I have, thought Jo.

Aloud, she said, 'Get them, and meet me at the bus station as soon as you can.'

'But—' Mark sounded ashamed. 'I'm not like you. I haven't got any money, Jo.'

Her heart clenched with pain for him. 'Don't worry, love,' she said gently. 'I have. I've been saving for this a long time.'

She waited at the bus station for hours. When

Mark came he was limping, and one side of his face was so badly bruised that his eye was closed. Jo's heart contracted in fierce protectiveness. But he grinned when he saw her.

'Got them,' he said, waving the small red book at her.

She hugged him swiftly. 'Did you have trouble getting away?'

He shrugged. 'Brian's out cold and Carol was shopping. They think I haven't got anywhere to run to.'

The adult world didn't believe Mark any more than it had believed Jo.

'Where are we going?'

'First the ferry. Then, France,' said Jo, out of her new, beautiful certainty.

Mark sucked his teeth. 'To Mr Sauveterre?'

'Yes.'

Mark looked at her oddly. 'Oh.'

It looked as if Carol had told him the tale about her adolescent crush. Jo winced inwardly, but aloud she said in a steady voice, 'Jacques is married now. He said we'd always be welcome.'

She bought their tickets at the big bus station and they embarked on an adventure of long-distance buses and ferries, crowded with families going on holiday. Mark talked cricket with a father and son, while Jo tried out her careful French. She was astonished to find the crew speaking back to her as if they understood.

After Boulogne there were more buses, slower and cosier—and a lot chattier. Then a lift from a kindly lorry driver. By that time Jo was rattling away easily in French. Even Mark was inserting a grunted comment or two.

This is going to *work*, Jo thought.

She had not realised how deeply pessimistic she had been. Not for herself, so much. After four years she knew she could survive pretty much anything if she kept her head. And she'd had a lot of practice in keeping her head by now. But she was scared for Mark. After all, he was a source of income for the Greys. Carol did not lightly let money pass out of her hands.

All through their journey Jo was alert for any sign of pursuit. But once they reached the Lot et Garonne she accepted it at last. No one was chasing them. They were home free.

In the little village they got directions to the Sauveterres' organic smallholding.

They walked along a small winding path that climbed a hillside, golden in the evening. The French countryside opened green arms to them.

The sun turned the quiet road to gold dust between the hedges.

And when they got to the Sauveterres' property Jacques hugged them as if they had just got back from Antarctica.

'I have always had such a conscience about leaving you two behind in that rainy place,' he said, ruffling Mark's hair.

Though he smiled, Jo thought from the look in his eyes that he meant it.

Over the years, Jacques had forgotten all about her teenage crush. He and his pretty, kind wife Anne Marie welcomed their unannounced visitors without reservation. Mark could stay with them as long as he wanted, they said. They pressed Jo to stay, too.

Jo said no. Not for more than a couple of nights.

Jacques might have forgotten her crush on him. But Jo hadn't. Blond Anne Marie was even prettier than the photograph he had sent. Prettier, and sweeter, and a petite five foot three. Also, just at that moment, six months pregnant.

Jacques was no longer a teacher. The Sauveterres were trying to make a living from their organic market garden. Their tumbledown farmhouse was wonderfully homely, but Jo knew about being hard up. Her sensitised antennae picked up lots of signs that money was tight. For all their kindness, the Sauveterres could not afford another mouth to feed. And anyway—

Whenever she thought about it, Jo hugged her arms across her breast defensively.

Well, Jacques and his Anne Marie were breath-takingly, idyllically happy. Every time they met—in the fields, in the kitchen, even on their way to and from the barn—they touched and kissed. And smiled into each other's eyes. Every gesture said *Look at us, see how in love we are.*

Jo did not wish them less in love. Of course she didn't. But pretty Anne Marie, with her soft flying hair and tanned, perfect legs, made Jo realise just how tall and plain she was herself. How unfeminine.

There was nothing to be done about it. Some people were just born unlovable. She accepted that. But, watching Anne Marie and Jacques—well, she minded.

'This,' said Jo, taking herself for an early-morning walk with the goats, 'is a bit of a shock.'

She had so focused on getting Mark away from the Greys that she had not thought about herself. Now she took stock, and it was like a douche of cold water.

She did not have to spend long in front of Anne Marie's mirror to see what the world saw: a six-foot scruff in combat trousers. Her nails were bitten. Her hair was a brown thatch like the rag doll scarecrow she'd had as a very small child. Her tee-shirt had holes. Her shoulders were as broad as Jacques's. No one was ever going to put their arm lovingly round shoulders like that.

'And just as well,' said Jo, aloud and firm. Aloud and firm usually helped. 'Love makes you weak. You can't afford that, Jo Almond.'

She wandered down the hillside, attended by curious goats. 'I am happy,' she told herself firmly.

It sounded good. And it was—nearly—true.

'I have never been this happy before.'

And that was certainly true.

Suddenly Jo grinned, stretching her arms above her head. 'It's a start,' she said gleefully. 'It surely is a start.'

It was more than a start. Within a week she had a job, and a place to stay, too.

It came about by pure chance. She was in the local market town, trawling round the businesses to see if anyone needed a waitress, a storeroom hand, a messenger. The square had cobbles and stone arcades and a balcony that looked as if the

Black Prince should be standing on it in full armour, making an arousing speech. To her amusement, she saw that a small crowd had gathered round some object of fascination.

Not the Black Prince, though. Approaching, she found they were grouped about an elderly open-topped Rolls Royce. It was shunting backwards and forwards between a medieval wall and the end of a colonnaded arcade, driven by a young Englishman getting more flustered and profane by the minute. People had even taken seats in the café opposite to enjoy the show.

Jo propped herself up against the wall and watched, too.

The driver was not much older than herself. He had a Caribbean tan which just might be natural, and expensively streaked hair which certainly wasn't. Her lips twitched. She folded her arms and waited.

'Look,' he said to the assembled market-goers. 'This isn't helping. Do any of you know how to—? Oh, damn.' This last as the car hiccupped forwards and grazed one of the columns.

Jo took pity on him. She strolled across and leaned on the driver's door.

'Drive her much, do you?'

He glared. 'She's my brother's. I was bringing

her down for a grease and a spray. But I took a wrong turning and ended up in the damned square.' He looked with loathing at the medieval buildings as if they were personal enemies.

She opened the door. 'Let me. I've driven big and old before.'

One of the bonuses of those long-ago car maintenance classes had been that she'd got to drive a lot. None of those cars had been an aristocratic Rolls, but they had been old and cranky—and some of them had been very big. She had no doubt that she could move the car without demolishing the picture-postcard corner.

She was right.

The Rolls came gently to rest in front of the café. The audience at the tables gave a small, polite round of applause. The rest of the crowd dispersed now the fun was over. The young man recovered his temper and thrust out a hand.

'How did you do that?' he said, in what appeared to be genuine awe. And, before she could answer, 'Crispin Taylor-Harrod. Oh, boy, did you save my bacon. Can I buy you a drink?'

Jo accepted coffee. Soon she was sitting beside him in the sunshine, sipping the headily fragrant stuff that bore no relation at all to the mid-morning brew of her last employer.

'What a bit of luck, bumping into you. I knew it was no good calling the garage to come and help. Old Brassens hates driving anything with right-hand drive. What are you doing round here?'

Jo told him. Well, not everything, obviously. Nothing that would put Mark or the Sauveterres at risk if Carol and Brian had organised pursuit. Just enough to make pleasant conversation in the sunshine before she went back to the serious business of tracking down a living wage.

Crispin frowned when she finished. 'You want a job? Seriously?'

'Yes,' said Jo simply.

'And you don't mind what you do?'

'No. Well,' she amended hurriedly, 'within reason. No go-go dancing, no brain surgery.'

He laughed, but his eyes were narrowed as if he were thinking deeply.

'And you know about old cars?'

Jo was taken aback. 'I know about old bangers. Nothing in the league of a Roller.'

He dismissed that with a wave of the hand. 'Yes, but you know about gearsticks and double de-clutching and stuff. You could drive them if you had to move them in and out of a garage, say?'

Jo agreed gravely that she did and she could.

'Do you *like* cars?' He sounded as if it were virtually impossible.

Jo thought about it. 'Yes, on the whole. They don't make promises and they don't let you down unless they can't help it. They don't spring many surprises as long as you look after them.'

'Ah,' he said. 'Would you like to?'

'Like to what?'

'Look after them?'

'Look after—' She broke off, staring at the gleaming aristocrat parked in front of the café. *'Them?* How many Rollers do you have, for heaven's sake?'

'Not me. My brother, Patrick. He has a collection.'

'Well, if he's a collector he must want to look after them himself.'

'Inherited,' said Crispin simply. 'He's going to sell them all. He told me to come here and take a look. He's got some expert coming from Rouen to put the cars back into running order. I'm supposed to be his little helper on the spot. But—well, it's not really my bag, and I've had an invitation to do some sailing up the coast of Spain. So I wondered…' He looked at Jo speculatively. 'I'd pay you.'

'I'm not qualified,' protested Jo.

Crispin laughed heartily. 'Good Lord, neither am I. You just have to book in the experts and take notes. I've got all the contact details. And it would get me out of prison.'

'Prison!'

But prison in Crispin Taylor-Harrod's terms turned out to be a fifteenth-century château, complete with turrets and a world-famous garden, albeit run down. The trouble was...

'It's miles from anywhere. No girls.'

Also no transport, no nightclubs, no bands.

'And my mate Leo has asked me on a boat which is wall-to-wall babes in bikinis,' said Crispin dreamily. 'Sex and sangria—that's what I need. Bit of beach life. Not a load of rusting radiators that haven't been out on the public road in twenty years.'

'It seems to me,' said Jo, torn between laughter and the first stirrings of hope, 'that you weren't the ideal choice for the job.'

Crispin grinned unrepentantly. 'Ah, but I came first. There was a bit of unpleasantness at college, and my mother threw me out. My brother Patrick said I could come here and do something useful. But what he really meant was stay out of trouble and do some revising.'

'You can't pay me to do that,' said Jo, disappointed.

'Oh, I've done all the revising. Nanny Morrison saw to that.' He tapped his teeth with the little coffee spoon. 'And now I want to get me some trouble before it's too late and I have to go back to school.' His face fell suddenly. 'Nanny Morrison. I'd forgotten. Blast and botheration.'

'What?'

'My brother Patrick doesn't employ women,' said Crispin simply. 'On principle. Nanny doesn't count. But nothing under fifty need apply.'

'That's illegal,' said Jo, affronted.

Crispin shrugged. 'Patrick's house. Patrick's law.'

Jo bristled. 'Nobody is above the law.'

Crispin gave a crack of laughter. 'You should meet my brother Patrick.'

'He sounds extremely arrogant,' she said crushingly.

'Yup. Arrogant, bullying, absolutely no feeling for a young man in his prime, and a hotshot wizard at just about everything.'

'Revolting,' she said, from the heart.

'Yes, but he's a good guy really,' said Crispin, changing tack with surprising suddenness. 'He likes his own way, but he's not mean with it. Last year he was up for some big award—the Ajax Prize, or something—and when he got it my ma wanted him to go off with a load of big cheeses to celebrate. But he said he didn't get to the States often and he wanted to spend time with his brother. So he came out clubbing with me and the boys instead.' He smiled reminiscently. Then his face darkened. 'Pulled all the talent in sight, too. Me and the boys didn't stand a chance.'

Jo sniffed. Patrick Taylor-Harrod could be a love god in person. She would still detest him. His stupid prejudice stood between her and the job of a lifetime.

'But it's so *unfair*. I could do this job.'

'Well, nobody argues with Patrick,' said Crispin fatalistically. 'Nanny Morrison would have you out in minutes. She reports to Patrick about *everything*.'

'Ah. I wondered how she'd got you to revise,' said Jo unwarily.

He chuckled, unoffended. 'Oh, well. It was a nice idea while it lasted. Drive me to the garage? Then you can meet her. She'll probably ask you up for tea and a swim. Grab it. Her teas are worth it.'

Jo laughed and went with him. But there was

a little sting in the invitation as well. Crispin had made it plain that he was desperate for a girl to flirt with—and Jo didn't even figure on his radar. He liked her. He was grateful to her. He was happy to throw one of Nanny's teas in her direction, with the careless hospitality of the inherited rich. But she was not flirt-worthy.

Oh, well, it only confirmed what she already knew, she told herself.

And worse was to come. Or better, depending on which way you looked at it.

Mrs Morrison, who looked more like a jobbing gardener than a nanny, wore substantial cotton shorts and a shirt, and, more importantly, huge bottle-bottom glasses. As Crispin had predicted, she took one look at his companion and said, 'Would you like to bring your friend back to the house for lunch, Crispin?' And then, not at all as he had predicted, and stunning Crispin and Jo alike, 'He would be very welcome.'

Crispin barely faltered. 'That would be great, Nanny. He's at a loose end right now,' he said smoothly.

Jo was not as quick as he was. Her mouth opened and shut. No sound came out.

He?

He?

'Work with me here,' breathed Crispin.

'But—'

'I'll show you the cars,' he said loudly. 'You're going to love them.' Then he was shoving her into the back of an old truck. 'Don't argue. This could be just what we need.'

'But—'

He thrust an industrial-sized bag of flour at her. 'Shut up.' He raised his voice. 'Ready when you are, Nanny.'

The truck rattled off at speed. They lurched and clung to the sides.

'Hell's teeth, she shouldn't be driving this thing,' said Crispin, momentarily side-tracked. 'If she thinks you're a boy she must be as blind as a bat.'

'Thank you,' said Jo hollowly.

'But, as she does, she's not going to be bleating to Patrick about you.'

'But other people will know I'm a girl.'

'The only other person around is old George, her husband. He's in a wheelchair. You can keep out of his way easily enough.'

'What if your brother comes back, though?'

That gave Crispin pause, but only for a moment. 'He's off war-reporting at the moment. Won't be home any time soon. And when he does get leave he goes to London or Washington or Paris. Definitely one for metropolitan amusements, my brother Patrick. Not a run-down château in rural France. It is so very rural. Besides, even the wine isn't up to his standard here. Not a *premier cru* in sight.'

'Then why on earth did he buy it?' said Jo, unreasonably annoyed with the unknown Patrick all over again.

'Didn't. Also inherited,' said Crispin absently. 'Look, the way I see it, you just fill in here for me for a month. I'll pay you cash. So your name never gets into the books. No one will ever know.'

'A month?'

He grinned. 'I'll be all partied out by then. If Patrick does visit it will be at the end of the vacation to check that I've followed orders. I'll be back from my babe and beach fest by then. You can slip off. He need not know you even existed.'

'It sounds wonderful,' said Jo, with longing.

A month would give her time to look round for a proper job, not just waiting tables or scrubbing floors. A month in this heavenly place, where poppies bobbed in the hedgerow and the long evening shadows were warm and smelled of herbs!

'Done,' said Crispin.

But she still held out. It seemed nasty, lying to

Mrs Morrison because the poor woman couldn't see properly. But, then again, Mrs Morrison wasn't the one who had set up this stupid interdiction on female workers. Patrick Taylor-Harrod positively *deserved* to be lied to.

And then she saw the Bugatti. She was old and dusty, and her front number plate hung off at a crazy angle. She was beautiful. It was love at first sight.

She could just about resist the scented nights and poetic turrets, thought Jo wryly. The unloved car was irresistible.

'Okay,' she said. 'Let's just hope arrogant Patrick stays where he is, that's all.'

'No worries,' said Crispin blithely. 'He won't be back home until the war is over. Once Patrick is onto a hot story, he never gives up.'

Jo banished her misgivings and tried a joke. 'I'll just have to make sure he never sees me as a hot story, then.'

Crispin went on laughing at that for a long time.

CHAPTER TWO

IT WAS a heavenly day and a heavenly place. Jo stopped in the middle of the little eighteenth-century bridge and looked around. She sighed with pleasure.

The willows almost met over the stream below. Bees murmured in the wild roses that clustered at the end of the decorative stone bridge and tumbled down the slope of the bank. The warm scented air was still. Only the occasional plop of some insect hitting the water disturbed the perfect silence. She was quite alone.

Jo shut her eyes, hardly daring to believe it was real. Less than a month ago she had been trawling for extra work among Manchester's cleaning agencies and late-night pizza bars, always worried about Mark. And now Mark was safe and she was in France.

France!

A France, what was more, that was straight out

of the fairytales. A France where there were fields of lavender and hillsides of sunflowers, their big faces following the sun as it crossed the sky; fortified medieval towns on the hilltops, like something out of a *Book of Hours*; little fast silvery rivers that fed the great golden swathe of the Garonne; grass that was so green it hurt the eyes. Warmth. Light.

Jo sighed. The summer sun filtered through the leaves and lay soft against her bare arms. It touched all her vulnerable places—under her hair, behind her ear, the base of her throat where the pulse beat. Touched then with the tiny assured kisses of a lover. When she closed her eyes it warmed her eyelids. All the locals wore sunglasses to protect them against the glare, but not Jo. For her the sun was a treasure.

Warmth, light and *safety*.

She opened her eyes. The fairytale landscape shimmered a little in the heat haze but it did not disappear. She breathed in the soft scents of summer: hot herbs, an elusive honeysuckle perfume on the breeze, grass.

'I am happy,' she said aloud. 'I am *so* happy.'

She recalled the heady perfection of the roses George had brought her this morning. He had wheeled himself into the neglected rose garden to cut them himself, and had brought them to her with the dew still on their softly crowded petals.

'Well, almost happy.'

There was a hint of wormwood in the perfect mix, of course. All her own fault, too. The lie that she had told seemed nastier every day. For the Morrisons had taken her to their hearts as if she were family.

At first Jo had followed Crispin's advice and tried to stay away from them. But Mrs Morrison cooked her little treats and left them on the work bench in the garage. And George, tooling round the grounds in his wheelchair, showed her all the neglected walks and copses of the place that he could reach. When he said how much he loved fishing, and how sad he was that he could no longer get his chair to the river, it had only been civil to find a path and wheel him down there.

Well, that was what Jo had told herself. The truth was, of course, that she was beginning to love the Morrisons. She loved the way Nanny's face lit up when Jo scratched shyly on the kitchen door. She loved the way George wheeled himself to meet her, full of some discovery he had made during the day. They *liked* her. After the superior expert from Rouen had arrived, shuddered, and left again, they had formed a sort of club. Jo basked in it as much as in the sunshine.

More and more, she wanted to tell them the truth. But how could she?

Hey, guys! Guess what? I was a girl all the time!

It was impossible, even for the sake of her conscience. She might just as well say Nanny was blind and George was stupid. So she kept quiet.

And most of the time she could forget it. She ran a grubby hand through her ragged chestnut hair, newly chopped by herself into a boyish crop. There were compensations, she reminded herself. Lots of them. A place of her own—and no shared bathroom or metered heating. Unbelievably, a job she was good at, and getting better at by the day! Even—oh, blissful thought—a library.

At the thought, Jo felt her lips stretch in a grin that was pure childish glee. A whole library to play in! This place was heaven.

She sometimes thought that the worst thing about her years as a runaway was how far it had kept her from books. She had never owned a book. Except for *The Furry Purry Tiger*, of course, she thought, with a choke of sudden laughter.

She said aloud, 'Tiger said, in his furry purry

voice, "Look into my eyes, my dears. How can you resist me?"' She gave a little skip of pure delight.

No, notwithstanding her own stupidity, the lie was only a slight shadow over her bliss.

'Blow nearly. I am *completely* happy,' she said aloud.

The sound of her own voice brought her up short. She looked round, embarrassed. But the birds sang undisturbed. The cicadas scissored away. And the landscape, under its shimmer of afternoon heat haze, was deserted.

'Still, that's no reason to go on standing in the middle of the road,' she scolded herself, adding with wry self-mockery, 'You never know when life is going to zap you again.'

Laughing, she went to the elegant parapet and leaned her elbows on the warm stone. Below her, a dragonfly was skimming the gold-shot water. Jo gave a deep, delighted sigh.

'But just at the moment I've got nothing left to wish for.' She breathed in the warm, scented air. 'Better enjoy it while it lasts.'

The little parcel Mrs Morrison had asked her to collect from the farm bumped against the stone as she moved. Jo made a face, reminded. Well, perhaps there *was* something to wish for.

She could wish that she knew exactly where

Patrick Taylor-Harrod was—and that he would not pop up like the demon king in a pantomime and spoil everything.

Crispin made him sound very demon king-ish: casual, arrogant, and quite without heart. Even Mrs Morrison, who was as fond of him as only a former nanny could be, admitted that no woman was safe from her Mr Patrick's charm. Though she also claimed that was largely their own fault, because they flung themselves at him.

Not that Jo would have flung herself at him. Or that arrogant elder brother Patrick would have taken her up on her offer if she had, Jo thought dryly.

At the thought, her eyes lit with sudden laughter. Maybe there were some advantages to being a sexless maypole, after all. It sounded as if arrogant Patrick was used to an altogether higher class of sexual harassment than she could offer.

She peered over the edge of the bridge at her reflection. Years of living from hand to mouth had left her with dramatic hollows under her cheekbones and a chin as pointed as a witch's, she thought disparagingly.

The water did not do justice to the depth and expressiveness of the strange greeny-brown of her eyes, of course. Nor did it reflect the long curling eyelashes or the exquisite softness of her skin. Jo would not have noticed if it had. All she saw was what she always saw when she could not avoid looking at her reflection. A stick-thin scarecrow with shoulders like a wardrobe. Carol had been right about that, at least.

Jo surveyed the dark rippling mirror dispassionately. She could not blame anyone for thinking she was a boy, she thought. And a boy she must stay—until Crispin came back.

She shook her shoulders and leaned further over the edge of the warm stone. The water looked inviting. And the sun was like an animal, a big friendly puppy, butting gently against the bare skin of her arms, saying, *Come and play.*

She had no swimsuit with her. She had not even owned one since primary school. But the little river was on private land, and the landscape was deserted. Wheelchair-bound Mr Morrison was resting, Mrs Morrison was waiting indoors for a phone call. Crispin was somewhere off the coast of Spain.

And it was a day made for swimming. Jo had not swum for years. Even then it had been in a municipal pool that smelled of chlorine. She had never swum in a river, with bees humming and the air full of the scent of grass and wild flowers.

It was irresistible.

Under a tangle of hazel bushes Jo found the narrow stone steps that spiralled down from the bridge. They were old and worn, covered in moss and lichen. She took off her shoes, feeling the warm moss under her toes in delight. Then she slipped down the curved stairs to the bank.

She lodged her package between the roots of a willow in deep shade, then quickly stripped off her clothes and left them where they fell. Her body was white and thin in the dappled shade. Thin, but tough, Jo thought cheerfully, shaking out her arms and dancing her bare feet in delight on the moss. Then she took a little run at the water and dived cleanly.

The dive made hardly a sound. But it was enough to alert the man.

He was leaning up against the bark of a willow on the opposite bank, completely hidden under the umbrella of its drooping branches. He had his hands in his pockets and his head bent. He was wearing a grim, bitter expression. At the faint splash, he looked up in quick offence.

This bridge was on private land! Nobody should be here! Behind his dark glasses, annoyance flickered uncontrollably.

Jo was unaware of the watcher. She was utterly caught up in the delight of the moment. She swam and turned and somersaulted in the water, laughing aloud with pleasure.

The man in the shadows watched, suddenly arrested.

She batted the surface of the water with her hands, making rainbow droplets fly up like a fountain. She shook her face in them, revelling in the sensation. Then she submerged completely and swam through the arch of the bridge.

The man took his hands out of his pockets and came to the edge of the bank, looking keenly after her. The fall of the willow would still have hidden him from Jo even if she had suspected that he was there. But she was enjoying herself too much to sense that she was being watched.

She streaked down to the bend in the river, where it was deeper and the water flowed faster. Then she turned in a neat dive and stroked lazily downstream again, on her back, looking at the clear sky through the tracery of overhanging leaves. She turned her head on the water to watch the bank dreamily. There were little patches of green-gold, where the sun streamed through unimpeded, areas of black shadow, like the cool place where she had left her clothes, and long stretches where the sun filtered through the trees as if it was creeping in round the edge of a mask, printing a sharp, delicate pattern of black lace on the turf.

She drew a deep breath, did a backward somersault into the weedy depths and disappeared. Instinctively, the man stepped out of the curtain of the willow, scanning the unbroken surface of the water.

Still unaware, Jo came up, shaking the water out of her hair and eyes, laughing. And it was then that she saw the bird, in a flash of emerald and blue, skimming the surface of the stream and flying away into the trees.

Jo went quite still. She stood where she was, the water up to her waist, tilting her head to watch the little creature. It had found a branch and was sitting there with whatever it had caught. She could make out the flash of a beady eye and the amazing jewel colours of the feathers.

She had heard of kingfishers. Seen pictures. But nothing had prepared her for this—this living iridescence, so small and yet so brilliant that it hurt the eyes. She held her breath.

Behind her, a voice said harshly, 'Have you hurt yourself?'

Jo was so absorbed she was not startled, much less embarrassed by her nakedness. She was hardly aware of it, she was concentrating so hard.

'Hush,' she said, the softness of her voice failing to disguise the clear note of command. 'That has to be a kingfisher.'

She was aware of movement behind her, as if whoever it was had been on the very edge of the bank and was now retreating a few paces.

'Where?' The voice was no less harsh, though this time it was scarcely above a whisper.

Jo raised a bare arm and pointed. Water fell from her fingers and elbow in a sparkle of silver.

'You look like a statue in a fountain,' the harsh voice said abruptly.

But Jo did not notice. The kingfisher was on the wing again. It streaked past them, a flash of sapphire and jade fire, and was lost in the foliage at the bend of the river.

Jo expelled a long breath.

'Oh, wasn't that *wonderful?*' she said, turning to face the voice.

It was a shock.

He was tall and slender, with an alarming air of compact, confident strength. He had a thin, proud face, which most women would probably call handsome. And his eyes were masked by the ubiquitous dark glasses. Jo registered all this in the blink of an eyelid and it left her unmoved.

And then he took his glasses off. And she froze to the spot as if he had cast a spell on her.

His eyes! They were deepset, under heavy brows. At first she thought they were black, then brown, then a strange golden yellow like old brandy. And they were staring at her as if she was an apparition from another world.

He was the first to speak.

'Well,' he said softly. All the harshness was gone, as if it had never been.

Jo shook her head a little, trying to break that mesmeric eye contact. Her ragged hair was plastered to her head, darkened to coal-black, all its red lights doused in the soaking it had received. The movement sent trickles of water from the rats' tails down her shoulders and between her breasts.

'I didn't realise anyone was there,' she said blankly.

At once she was furious with herself. Stupid, *stupid*, she thought. Of course you knew he was there—the moment he spoke. And of course you didn't know before that, or you would not have been jumping about in the water with no clothes on.

Realisation hit her then. She gave a little gasp and plunged her shoulders rapidly under the water. But she couldn't quite break the locking of their gaze.

He smiled a little. 'I didn't intend that you should.'

Jo digested that. 'You were *spying* on me?' she said, incredulous.

It did not seem likely, somehow; it was out of character with that haughty profile, she thought. Years of living on her wits had taught Jo to sum up people fast. She was not usually wrong.

His face reflected distaste. 'Quite by accident.'

He sounded so weary that Jo flushed, as if it were she, not he, who was at fault. She was indignant.

'How do you spy on someone by accident?' she demanded hotly.

He smiled again, startling her. It was a sudden slanting of that too controlled, too uncompromising mouth and it changed his face completely. Suddenly it was not just other women who would have called him handsome. And more than handsome.

Disconcerted, Jo swallowed. And huddled deeper under the water.

He said, 'I was here first. I saw you come down from the bridge. By the time I realised you were intending to strip off and leap into the water it was too late to warn you that you were not alone.'

'Oh.'

He relented. 'But I admit I watched you playing in the water. I suppose a gentleman would have gone away. But you looked so—happy.'

The mouth was a thin line again. Not so much harsh, Jo thought in sharp recognition, as holding down a pain of the soul that was scarcely endurable. She knew something about that.

She said gently, 'It's the place. Anyone would be happy here.'

His eyes held hers. There was a little silence. For a moment even the bees stilled in the summer air. He shook his head slowly, as if this time he was the one under a spell—and trying desperately to break free.

'Only if you're very young.'

Jo thought of those years—in shabby rooms when she'd had some money, sleeping in bus shelters and an old boat-house by a canal when she hadn't. Of cold, and intermittent hunger, and the need to stay painfully alert against theft and worse. The longing for a bath. The loneliness. The need to stay lonely because you never knew who you could afford to trust.

'I'm not that young,' she said dryly.

He looked up, arrested. Then seemed to pull himself together. He almost shrugged.

'You look about sixteen.'

'Nineteen. But experience speeds up the clock.' And she looked at him very straightly.

Something seemed to stir, shift in his eyes. Something—she did not know what—half physical sensation, half a strange emotion that made her want to abandon good sense and laugh and cry at once, seemed to wake in Jo in answer. Bewildered, she knew she had never felt anything like it before. All she knew was that it reached out to whatever was waking in him.

Then, like a snake striking, it arced between them. Eyes widening in shock, she realised it had taken him by surprise as much as it had her. He looked shaken.

Jo gasped and sat down suddenly on the riverbed. The water closed over her head. She thought the man winced. She saw his head go back as if at a blow. But she was too busy expelling water to be sure.

When she came up she was spluttering. She shook the water away and looked at him. He was hunkered down on the bank. But now he was laughing.

It changed his face completely, emphasising those startling good looks. It made him look like a fully paid-up heartthrob, she thought sourly, rubbing water out of her eyes.

In some ways it was a relief that the grim look had gone. So had that electric awareness. That should have been a relief too. Yet, if she was honest, Jo did not know whether she was glad or sorry. On the whole, she thought, it was probably just as well.

And yet… And yet…

He said, 'Hadn't you better come out and get dry? You don't look very safe.'

Putting her disturbing reflections away from her, Jo shook her damp head vigorously. 'I'll have to run around to get dry,' she warned him cheerfully. 'No towel.'

The man's look of amusement deepened.

'An impulse bathe, then?'

She looked guilty. 'I just saw the water and couldn't resist.'

He shook his head. 'Dangerous.' But he was still laughing.

Jo liked him laughing at her. She decided to tease him back. 'Giving in to your impulses is dangerous?'

'Usually.'

He stood up and shrugged off his dark jacket. He was wearing a soft navy shirt underneath, open at the neck. Without bothering to undo the buttons, he hauled it over his head and held it out to her.

'There you are—dry yourself on that.'

His chest was a lot paler than his face. There was a dusting of dark hair along the ribs. Jo's mouth dried. This sudden nakedness seemed to give off a primitive heat. And he looked so *strong*.

She stepped back, but the water resisted. The little river seemed to be pushing her towards him. She fought not to look. She did not know why. It had something to do with getting herself back under control.

Am I out of control, then?

Despising herself, she said hurriedly, 'That's very kind of you, but I don't need it. Really.'

'*You* might not,' he said with wry self-mockery. 'I'm not sure how much of your running around to get dry my self-control could take.'

'Oh,' said Jo, completely taken aback.

So the awareness was still there after all. Just coated lightly with good manners. Jo did not know a lot about manners, but she was certain that this man knew all there was to know. He had decided they were civilised strangers meeting in unusual circumstances. And he had almost convinced her that was all they were. Almost.

Her eyes fell. She felt shamefaced, yet oddly excited.

'Go on—take it,' he said. 'In weather like this, I can certainly spare it.'

She nodded, not lifting her eyes. As quickly as the water would allow, she waded forward and took it from him. Their fingers did not touch.

Was that because it was me being careful not to touch? Jo wondered. Or was it his decision? And was that good manners? Or something else?

She held the shirt high out of the water and waded back to the other bank. Putting one hand on the bank, she vaulted lightly up onto it and disappeared among the trees. The shirt was linen, soft against her tingling skin. In fact, her whole body was tingling, her bones, muscles and nerves and all.

Ridiculous, Jo told herself. Because of a man I've never seen before and won't again?

But she fluffed up her damp hair before she climbed back up the stone steps and emerged into the sunlight.

He was waiting for her. He had strolled along the bank and up the other set of steps. Now he was leaning on the stone coping, looking upriver.

'It's beautiful, isn't it?' Jo said, approaching softly.

Even more ridiculous, now that she had her clothes on she felt shy. It was crazy. She was never shy. And she had talked to him without constraint when he'd surprised her cavorting naked in the stream. So why this crushing embarrassment now?

With a great effort she met his eyes and gave him what she hoped was a friendly smile without complicated shadows. From his wry look she wasn't sure she had succeeded.

She thought suddenly, *There's a game going on here. He knows how to play it and I don't.*

But all he said was, 'Yes, beautiful. It's also private. How did you find your way here?'

'Oh, I've been to the farm,' Jo said, with a wave at the distant farmhouse.

'Ah. The old back drive. I see.'

'No one uses it,' she assured him, blushing at the criticism she detected. 'I was sure I was alone.'

'So was I,' he said with a sharp sigh. 'It seems we were both wrong.'

It occurred to her that he might have wanted to be alone with his thoughts. That harsh voice had not sounded happy. Suddenly she felt less shy.

'I'm sorry,' she said with quick contrition. 'I know what it's like to want to get away from people. Were you fishing or something?' she added, remembering Mr Morrison's daily pilgrimages to the other river.

'No. Not fishing. Thinking. Trying to work out what to do—' He broke off, gritting his teeth.

Jo recognised that look. 'Ouch,' she said, with sympathy.

He gave a fierce shrug, as if he were angry with himself. 'I can normally find my way through things. But this time—there are just too many people getting in the way.'

Jo nodded. 'Been there,' she said, with feeling.

He was glaring at some unseen enemy. 'I doubt it,' he said impatiently.

She bit back a smile. 'You'd be surprised.'

He looked at her then. In fact he swung round on her, and the fierce look went out of his eyes.

'What?'

Jo was running her fingers through her wet hair.

'Other people have always been my biggest problem,' she said wryly and—to her own amazement—without bitterness. 'You just have to go round them. Or turn and face the enemy.'

'You're very wise for nineteen.' He sounded startled.

She shrugged. 'I told you. Experience puts a lot of extra miles on the clock.'

He leaned against the parapet, the curious golden-brown eyes searching her face.

'Yes, I can see that,' he said slowly. Almost as if he were thinking of something else.

Jo remembered *The Furry Purry Tiger*: those warm eyes that lured and lulled the tiger's victims. *Look deep into my eyes, my dears. Can you resist me?*

She gave a gasp and took two sharp steps backwards.

And the spell was broken.

The man looked at her frowningly. 'Who are you? What are you doing here?' he said in quite another tone. 'A student on some exchange?'

Jo realised for the first time, with a start, that he knew she was a girl. It was like a douche of cold water. Her face went blank.

The Morrisons spoke to her and about her as if she was a boy. The kindly farmer's wife accepted her as a boy. When she went into the bank, the bored counter clerks treated her as a boy.

And now here was someone who had the most precise and irrefutable evidence that she was a girl. And that she was English. If he asked in the neighbourhood the local people would recognise the English factotum looking after the château's antique cars, all right. And this stranger was now able to tell them that she was not everything they had thought.

Jo went cold.

'Sort of,' she muttered.

'And where did you learn about turning to face the enemy?' he asked in an idle tone.

Jo bit her lip, hardly paying attention. How could she have been such a fool? How *could* she?

'On the road, mostly,' she said absently.

Perhaps if she told him she was just passing through...

The black brows flew up. 'On the road? What does a student study on the road?'

Jo could have kicked herself. Yet another unwary detail let slip because she wasn't thinking clearly. This man was dangerous—or at least the effect he seemed to be having on her was dangerous. At this rate, she would talk herself right out of her magical new job.

She shook her damp hair, spraying droplets on his powerful naked chest. She saw his muscles contract as the water made contact and her heart gave a funny little lurch. Concentrate, she told herself. *Concentrate!*

'Life,' she said flippantly.

He frowned.

'I've heard about the university of life. But I've never heard of anyone selecting it,' he said dryly. 'What happened? Drop out of college?'

Jo gave a little laugh that broke. Her ruined education was one of the things that hurt most.

'Never got that far,' she said briefly.

The frown did not lift. 'Why not?'

She shrugged. 'Oh, this and that.'

'The open road looked more attractive?'

She thought about the night she had finally run away. Since then she had occasionally slept in railway stations and not had enough to eat, and there had been one or two hairy moments. But no one had set out to beat her senseless because he was in a bad temper and drunk. No one was going to, ever again.

'The open road looked more attractive,' she agreed quietly.

'On your own?'

She hesitated.

'Not any more?' he interpreted.

Jo shrugged.

He was persistent. 'Boyfriend pushed off?'

Jo said carefully, 'Mark is staying with some people he knows.'

'So it was you who decided to keep on moving?'

She gave a little laugh. 'Not much choice. They only had room for one, and Mark had first claim.'

His mouth twisted. 'So he's found himself a billet. Where does that leave you? Have you found somewhere to stay?'

Jo was unnerved by his curiosity. It stampeded her into an uncharacteristic lie.

'Not round here,' she said quickly.

'In one of the towns, then? How did you find your way to the river here? Just out for a day's picnic in the country?'

'Yes.'

She sounded curt and he looked surprised.

But she had told enough lies here. She did not want to contaminate this beautiful place, this moment, any more. For some odd reason she did not want to lie to this man, either. She began to edge away.

'Can I drive you somewhere? To join your friends, perhaps?' he said. 'I left my car on the road.'

'No,' she said, horrified.

But a bit of her mind noted that he seemed to be passing through, that he was not one of the locals who could inadvertently expose her deception. It was a relief.

His eyebrows flew up. She had sounded almost rude, Jo thought in despair.

'I mean, no, thank you,' she corrected herself.

'Hey,' he said, half gentle, half affronted, 'you don't have to be afraid of me. If I were that sort of villain I'd have already jumped on you.'

Jo winced. 'Sorry.'

Her voice was constrained, almost sulky. She hated it. She didn't want this man to think she was sulky. But it was better that he knew nothing more about her.

She went on hardily, 'I know where I'm going, and I'm not in any hurry.'

He looked at her searchingly. 'You'll be all right on your own?'

Her chin lifted. 'I always am.'

He gave a wry smile. 'I guess you are. Well, no more skinny-dipping, hmm? Not when you're on your own, anyway.'

'You mean, no more impulses,' Jo corrected him with a touch of bitterness.

His eyes narrowed. 'That would be a pity.'

Her head came up, suspicious.

He added, with quite unnecessary emphasis, almost as if he were reminding himself of something, 'At your age, I mean.'

She gave a little awkward nod. 'Okay.'

'And where will I find you?'

Alarm flared. Her head reared up again.

'What do you mean, find me?' she demanded sharply

'You're walking off with my shirt,' he pointed out, amused. 'It's rather a favourite. I'd like it back sometime.'

'Oh!' Jo looked down at the damp, crumpled linen she was still clutching. She thrust it at him. 'Here.'

This time their fingers did touch. He caught her hand and held it strongly. If he pulled it back to his body she would touch that warm naked chest with its dusting of hair and its steadily beating heart—and its frightening strength.

Jo's mouth dried. She stood very still.

He did not carry her hand to his body.

'Where are you staying?' he said again. This time it was not casual.

Jo was mute with misery. But she didn't dare tell him. A whole summer with a roof over her head, a job, close to Mark. She couldn't put it at risk. She *couldn't*.

When she met his eyes, her own were swimming in tears. She who never cried. She shook her head, denying him. It was the most difficult thing she had done in a long time.

He let her go and stepped back.

'As I said, you're very wise.'

His voice was light, hard. His smile did not reach his eyes.

For some reason it hurt. She felt almost as if she had let him down. But what choice did she have?

Run, said her inner voice.

She hated it. She was not afraid of him.

But she *was* afraid of his questions. And these days it was not just *her* safety that depended on her. She needed to make sure the Greys could not track down Mark through her. She could not afford to answer him.

She gritted her teeth. And, before the man could move to prevent her, she turned and fled back down to the riverbank. She ran until she lost herself among the trees.

And closed her ears to the voice calling her to come back. In case she did.

CHAPTER THREE

PATRICK shouted but the girl did not stop. He took a hasty step forward—and his damned leg nearly gave out. He stopped dead, leaning against the parapet swearing.

She swarmed up the bank as if the devil were after her. And there was not one single thing he could do to stop her! He pounded his fist against the traitor leg. But the thing was shaking. Of course, he had been standing on it too long. Just as he had been told not to.

Meanwhile, the girl slid back over the retaining wall like a contortionist. Futilely, he raised an arm. But she had her back to him and did not see it. Almost certainly she would not have responded, even if she had seen, he thought, berating himself as an idiot. She had made no bones about it, after all.

Then she was pelting away, out of his life.

He heard her footsteps die away. His hand fell.

Six months ago he would have followed her. Caught her, too. Today there was no point in even trying. By the time he got up the bank she would be out of sight.

'Damn!'

He limped painfully over the bridge. The tall, coltish figure was flying down the back drive towards the copse.

If only he could have caught her, thought Patrick grimly. He could have told her she was trespassing. And then he could have *made* her tell him her name. He was astonished at the fury of regret that he had not managed to get a name out of her.

'Must be losing my touch,' he told himself, trying for irony. 'Better go back to journalist school.'

He watched the rapidly diminishing figure. She must have scratched herself quite badly on those overhanging branches. But she did not let it slow her down. She did not look back, either, though he called out in the voice that had cut through gunfire and collapsing buildings.

Flying away from him down the deserted drive, she looked like a wild thing. Her disreputable old shirt flapped like the wings of a heron about to take off, oddly at one with the sun-drenched hillside.

He thought of the way she had played in the water, like a young otter. And how shocked she had been when she'd remembered she was naked. His mouth lifted at the memory.

You couldn't expect to tame a creature like that. No wonder she had fled. And just as well, he told himself firmly. She was a complication that he did not need, with her big hazel eyes and her shattering honesty.

But he still wished his leg worked well enough to catch her. Or that she had trusted him enough to give him a name.

And he wished—crazily, in the circumstances—that she had looked back. Just once. Just so that he knew he had not imagined that tingle of electricity in the air between them. Just so he knew she'd felt it, too.

Jo plunged off the back drive as soon as she could and ran into the copse. She crashed through the undergrowth. Her breath came in great gasps that sounded like sobs. The long sleeves of her lumberjack shirt saved her arms from the worst scratches, but flailing twigs caught her painfully across the face and neck. Her heart pounded under her ribs until she thought it would leap out of her body.

At last she could run no more. She stopped.

There was no sound of pursuit. The man had obviously not taken off after her.

For some reason, that surprised her. She could not quite believe it. He had not seemed like a man who would let himself be bested once he decided he wanted something.

And he had wanted her. She was sure of it. Maybe only for a moment, but she knew in her bones, in her blood, that it had been there. Only perhaps he had not wanted her enough.

She looked back warily, as if she were afraid that he would leap out from behind a willow. But she was alone with the birdsong and the still afternoon shadows. She was relieved, she told herself. Of course she was. Anything else would have been too complicated.

She dropped forward in an attitude of exhaustion, one arm against the trunk of a beech tree, her forehead propped against her closed fist.

This was crazy, she told herself. Running away like that was stupid. She had probably convinced him that she was a vagrant, if not worse. It was not even as if he had threatened her.

Jo caught herself, remembering the dazzling warmth of his hand. The warm, lifting chest, with its dusting of hair and overwhelming aura of power.

Okay, threatened her peace of mind maybe, she allowed with a wry grin. Her breathing calmed, returned to normal. She straightened.

All right. So the man had disturbed her. From what she had seen in his face, she had disturbed him too. So? It had happened. She wasn't going to see him again.

No big deal, Jo told herself fiercely. No big deal at all.

The man would get in his car and go on to Toulouse, or to Paris, or wherever it was he was bound when chance had brought him off the highway and into her life. There was no point in worrying about it. And she had avoided telling him who she was or where she was living. So there was no danger that he would reveal her deception to the Morrisons and thence to tyrannical Patrick Taylor-Harrod, wherever he was.

That was all that mattered. She held onto that piece of common sense for all she was worth. Her job and her room above the garage were safe. This unexpected flicker of regret was a small price to pay for it.

Jo lifted her head and looked about her. She had come away from the river. She was not certain where she was. She would have to go back to the bridge to get her bearings.

She looked down at her scratched hands. They were trembling slightly. It surprised her. She did not tremble easily. They were also empty.

'Eggs!' exclaimed Jo in horror, all thoughts of the dark man expelled. 'Mrs Morrison's shopping. Butter! Oh, my Lord!'

She made her way back almost as fast as she had come. When she got within sight of the river she slowed down and began to move cautiously. But there was no sign of the man, or the car he had talked about. This time when she told herself it was a relief, she had the grace to admit she was lying.

She was disappointed as hell.

Jo smiled wryly. She *should* be relieved. She would be this evening, when she had got her head back together again, she told herself. She was always good at putting her head back together after a crisis.

Putting the man out of her mind, she looked about for the small bag of shopping she had brought from the farm.

When she located it, it felt suspiciously squashy. The butter had taken on the shape of the tree roots which had been cradling it. Inside its greaseproof paper wrapping it had taken on the texture of warm toffee.

Great! Mrs Morrison would be justifiably

annoyed. Equally annoyed with herself, Jo made for the château at a quick trot.

The back drive was a rather grand name for the stony path that wound round the edge of the wood, through the paddock behind her barn, to the side door of the château. But there was a moment, just when you came out of the trees, when you looked across the fields and saw the château like a turreted palace out of a story book.

Jo never stopped marvelling at it. It was set on a promontory, almost an island, that jutted out into the river. It was a square building in parchment-coloured stone, simple except for its exuberance of conical roofs which crowned the turrets at each corner. She always thought that there ought to be knights on horseback, with their pennants flying, galloping up to the main entrance.

But today, as always, there was no one there. Just the simple building, drowsing in the afternoon sun, the gravel raked and unblemished in front of the fortress walls. No knights and ladies. No flags. The medieval romantic who had built it was long gone.

Jo laughed at her own imaginings and walked on again, swinging the maltreated shopping.

But when she got to the servants' door which she always used there was a visitor, after all.

She made a face. Visitors did not usually find their way round to the kitchen gardens and the courtyard across from her barn. Although they did come winding down the front drive from time to time, not realising that it was a private house. Usually they were hung about with cameras and guidebooks and wanted to be shown round. If they were well dressed enough and polite Mrs Morrison sometimes gave them a drink, even let them picnic in the grounds if they were tired.

Jo looked at the powerful black sports car with its top down and its cream leather seats baking in the sun. Definitely a candidate for a glass of wine under the trees, she thought, grinning. She slipped into the cool marble-floored corridor that led to the kitchen and began untying the string round the parcel.

She patted the butter back into something re-sembling a brick shape and put it in the fridge. She was just turning to the eggs when Mrs Morrison came in. She blinked her cloudy eyes at Jo and smiled. She was rather red in the face, but she looked pleased.

'Oh, such a to-do,' she said.

Jo often wondered how Mrs Morrison recog-nised that she knew someone. It must be the way they stood or moved, she thought. Even squinting hard, it was perfectly plain that she could not make out Jo's features. But she still knew who was standing in the kitchen when she came in.

Jo's conscience stirred again. She quelled it. If it were not for her, the Morrisons would be alone here now Crispin had gone. The man from Rouen who was supposed to be restoring two of the cars had taken one look at the distance between the château and the nearest town and got right back onto his motorbike.

So, she told herself, the Morrisons needed her. Not just to run errands to the farm, but to act as able-bodied backup. George Morrison was in a wheelchair and his wife could hardly see. Jo was necessary to them. But she still wished she could tell them she was a girl.

To put it out of her mind, she asked quickly, 'Visitors in need of the guided tour?' although she was not really interested.

Mrs Morrison, however, was. She looked pleased at having news to impart.

'Oh, no, nothing like that. You'll never believe it.' She paused. Mrs Morrison liked her big effects.

'What is it, then? Martians invaded?' asked Jo, humouring her.

'The master's back.'

'Back? Crispin?'

She was incredulous. Once Crispin had got her to agree to his wild scheme, he installed her in the barn, gave her the keys and the record books and taken off the same night. By now, Jo would have put money on his being on a Spanish beach with his friends and an endless supply of sangria. She had the impression that nothing short of an earthquake would get him back. He had been quite frank about life at the château—from Crispin's point of view, it was one step away from solitary confinement.

'Oh, no, not Crispin.' Mrs Morrison was just faintly scornful. 'The master. Mr Burns.'

'Who?' Jo had never heard the name before.

'Mr Burns.' The pride of an old nanny took over. 'My Patrick.'

The bottom dropped out of Jo's world. Arrogant Patrick! The elder brother who wouldn't have a woman on his staff.

She heard Crispin's voice in her head: *Patrick's house. Patrick's law.*

Her heart went into free fall and then landed with a sickening crunch at the bottom of a deep well. For the moment it was so dreadful she could not take it in.

Patrick Burns. Did she know the name from somewhere? It danced around maddeningly, just out of reach. But she was certain that it was nothing to do with the château.

She said, stupidly, 'But I thought his name was Taylor-Harrod. Crispin said *his* name was Taylor-Harrod.'

Mrs Morrison sniffed. 'Madam married Mr Taylor-Harrod when Patrick was eight. And then Count Orsini after that. And then—'

But Jo wasn't listening. All she could think was, Why the hell hadn't Crispin told her that he and his arrogant elder brother Patrick didn't share a surname?

And then reality began to set in.

Patrick Burns was back. Patrick Burns, who didn't want girls in the place and didn't yet know he was employing one. Patrick Burns, who presumably would not take kindly to being deceived. Patrick Burns, who, when last heard of at least, had been in possession of perfect eyesight as well as a high-handed determination to go his own way regardless of law or fairness.

Perhaps she could keep out of his way, thought Jo, feverishly calculating. Perhaps if she slouched around and only spoke in monosyllables he wouldn't notice that she was a girl any more than Mr Morrison or the people in the market had noticed.

She did not have much hope, but it was all she had to cling to. Perhaps he wouldn't stay long enough to notice the deception. Perhaps she wouldn't be found out.

And with another part of her brain she was thinking, I needn't have run away by the stream after all. I was going to be found out anyway. I could have told the dark man my name. I could have told him where to find me. I've spoilt it all for nothing.

She said hoarsely, 'What did he say when he found Crispin had gone?'

'He was a little put out,' admitted his fond nanny.

Jo thought about what Crispin had said and deduced that it meant ructions.

'He was really annoyed that the man from Rouen wasn't here, I can tell you,' Mrs Morrison went on, with relish. 'But after I explained he said he was pleased Crispin had found you to replace him. He said maybe Crispin was showing some sense at last.'

'Great,' Jo said in a hollow voice.

So, not only did he not expect a girl, he expected a fully paid-up professional motor restoration expert. Oh, boy, was this interview going to be fun!

In her head a mocking voice said, *Spoilt, spoilt, spoilt. All for a lie you needn't have told.* She shivered. She had always known lies were bad luck.

'And he wants to see you as soon as you come in.'

'Great,' she said again. And then, realising what the housekeeper had said, 'Wants to see *me*?'

Mrs Morrison looked surprised. 'Of course. He went straight over to the garage as soon as I told him. He looked through the record books. He was very impressed,' she added encouragingly. 'He said you really seemed to have got a grip on it in the last week. Those were his very words.'

'Oh,' said Jo. She swallowed.

'He's in the study now. Go along to him.'

Jo sought desperately for an excuse. She couldn't find one.

'I'm taking him in a brandy now,' said Mrs Morrison, who wouldn't have dreamed of letting the outdoor help touch her starched linen tray cloth. 'You can come along and open the door for me, like a good boy.'

There was no help for it. Jo shrugged. She had to face him sooner or later. She went.

She slouched along in Mrs Morrison's wake, trying to look like a gangly teenage boy. She opened the door for the housekeeper to pass through. Then, sticking her hands in her pockets and tucking her head against her chest, she followed.

She thought Patrick Burns would be at the desk, like a Victorian tyrant. He wasn't. He was standing at the tall window, looking out across the formal lawns in the direction of the river. He was very dark.

He wasn't dressed like a Victorian tyrant, either. Not even in a suit. Just dark trousers and a soft navy shirt. A crumpled navy shirt…

Mrs Morrison set the tray down on an occasional table.

A crumpled navy shirt. And she knew exactly how it had been crumpled.

Jo froze. This couldn't be happening.

'This is Jo, Patrick,' Mrs Morrison said to the tall back. 'The lad Crispin brought in to look after the cars.'

He turned. Jo found that her heart had not even been in sight of the bottom of the well before. She stared at him in horror.

His brandy-coloured eyes flared, then narrowed alarmingly. Jo thought she had never seen such a hard expression on anyone's face in her life. She took an involuntary step back at the sheer fury of it.

Then he said very softly, 'Is this a joke?'

It's *him*, Jo thought. And mixed with the horror was a sort of grieving exultation.

'I'm sorry?' Mrs Morrison said blankly.

'What are you doing here?' he rapped out at Jo, ignoring the housekeeper. He seemed hardly aware that she had spoken.

Jo's mouth felt as if it were full of sand. She had no voice to answer him.

Mrs Morrison began to look rather alarmed. 'I told you. He's the boy Crispin brought in. You said he'd done a good job with the cars,' she reminded him, her voice jumping.

Jo sympathised with the housekeeper's alarm. Patrick Burns looked thunderous.

His mouth twisted, curling up to one side in a devil's sneer. He was bitterly, furiously angry. But he did not raise his voice.

'So this is Crispin's doing. I might have known it.' Through the level tones Jo could hear anger licking up like flames catching hold.

She winced.

'He's been really helpful with George,' Mrs Morrison added, anxious. 'And he hasn't been a mite of trouble.'

'Not to you, perhaps,' said Patrick Burns with a flash of naked rage. His own reaction seemed to annoy him. He turned away abruptly and poured himself a brandy.

'Not to anyone,' the housekeeper said stoutly. 'Runs my errands. Pushes George back uphill when the motor on that nasty chair of his gives out. Keeps himself to himself over in the barn.'

Patrick raised his glass to his lips and looked at Jo over the rim. His mouth twisted.

'Keeps himself to himself?' he echoed. 'And lives over the shop, I suppose? I see. Clever. Very clever.'

Mrs Morrison was uneasy, and it showed. Jo felt indignant. It was hardly the housekeeper's fault that Crispin had brought her here under false pretences. Especially as Jo suspected that a good half of Patrick Burns's rage was because she had run away from him on the bridge. It was not fair to take his temper out on Mrs Morrison.

Her tongue seemed to twist itself in knots when she tried to say that, however. So she just glared at him instead.

At last, Patrick Burns seemed to notice his housekeeper's agitation.

'Sorry, Nanny,' he said, his voice softening. 'It's not your fault. Crispin has overreached himself this time. And he's not alone.' He sent Jo a narrow-eyed look that made her mouth go dry. But he patted Mrs Morrison on the shoulder. 'It's nothing to do with you. Don't worry about it.'

Mrs Morrison looked even more alarmed.

He managed to smile at the housekeeper, though Jo saw that it got nowhere near his eyes.

'No excuse for upsetting you, Nanny. Sorry. Jo—that is your name? Jo?—Jo and I will settle this between us. You go and get on with whatever you were doing. Jo and I need to talk.'

Mrs Morrison could hardly do anything but leave the room in face of a direct order. She sent Jo a puzzled, sympathetic look. And went.

Patrick Burns turned back to Jo. His eyes raked her up and down. It was about as pleasant as being rubbed over with sandpaper.

She tried to remember the warmth of that startling smile. His kindness when he gave her his shirt. The attraction that had flared between them.

But it was no good. He looked as if his face had been hacked out of stone. As if he hated her.

She could not imagine how she had ever thought that he had smiled at her. It must have been a trick of the light.

'Jo,' he said softly, tasting it.

She swallowed. She still could not think of anything to say.

'Short for Joanna? Josephine? Joelle?'

There was no point in trying to pretend that she did not know him, that he had made a mistake. She was even wearing the same stained lumberjack shirt. Besides, those bold, cold eyes were telling her that he remembered perfectly well the body under those clothes.

Oh, yes, the attraction was still there all right. Only now it was not exciting. It was a threat.

Jo felt the colour stain her cheeks at the insolence of that look.

'Joanne,' she muttered.

'Joanne what?'

She hesitated.

'No more pretty games,' Patrick Burns said softly. 'I don't find them amusing. If you don't answer me, I shall hand you over to the police.'

Her head lifted in a quick flare of alarm. If the police came they might be able to track Mark down through her. If Carol had had the gall to report him missing, of course. After Brian's violence, would she dare, though? The Greys had never reported it when Jo took off, she knew. She bit her lip, weighing the chances.

He watched her—and, inevitably, misinterpreted her reaction.

'So you're wanted by the police too, are you, my wild thing?'

The endearment was a deliberate insult, and he wanted her to know it. She stiffened, surprisingly hurt. He was shattering a stupid fantasy— one she had hardly recognised until now. But it had been there from the moment he touched her fingers. She set her teeth and refused to react.

'Your name,' he rapped out.

Jo swallowed and said quietly, 'You needn't shout. It's Jo Almond.'

'So you gave Crispin your real name? Interesting. How long have you known him?' He paused. 'Was it because of *you* that he sent the Rouen guy packing?'

He shot the questions at her like a machine gun. Or, she thought with a strange little sadness, like an interrogator who hated her.

But at least they were questions she could answer factually. Without expression, she did so.

'I met Crispin in town. It was chance.' She

shrugged helplessly. 'I didn't know him before. He got the Rolls into a pickle and I helped him out. So…' She spread her hands. 'He offered me the job of covering for him while he was on holiday. I needed one. So I said yes. I was supposed to be a gopher for the expert when he arrived, just like Crispin was. That was all.'

Patrick Burns said, in a voice like glass, 'It's so unlikely I almost believe it.'

Jo lifted her head with sudden pride. 'You said yourself I've looked after the cars well.'

He let out an expletive that shocked her. He saw her recoil and his mouth twisted.

'We are not talking about cars, sweetheart. You're not stupid. You know what we're talking about.'

Jo could feel the hot, painful build-up of tears. That didn't often happen, and it made her *mad*. She averted her eyes and tried to sniff quietly.

'You mean the fact that I deceived the Morrisons?' she said desolately.

He put his glass down.

'And the fact that you deceived me.' It was said quietly. But the tone was virulent.

Jo blenched.

She stammered, 'I never m-meant to. I didn't know who you were.'

'I suppose I should be grateful for that,' he mused. His tone was savage, for all his attempted lightness. 'What would you have done if you had known, I wonder?'

Jo stared. 'Told you the truth, of course,' she said, bewildered. 'There would have been no point in doing anything else.'

For a moment she almost told him how she'd hated lying. That she regretted running away from him the moment she had done it. But his expression was much too grim. He would not believe her.

'So tell me now,' he said softly.

His eyes were like lasers. Jo shifted uncomfortably, but her chin came up in defiance.

'The whole truth,' he warned. 'Not just a careful selection to keep me sweet.'

Jo bared her teeth. 'Wouldn't dare.' But she didn't sound frightened, she thought thankfully. She sounded defiant. And mocking.

He ignored the defiance. 'Good decision.'

Patrick had not invited her to sit down, but she did anyway. She chose a narrow, high-backed chair with a *petit point* seat set on the very edge of a priceless rug. It was deeply uncomfortable and no doubt very valuable. The furniture in this house, Crispin had told her, was even more antique than the cars.

Suddenly, gratefully, she was angry at the waste of it.

'If I had all this money I'd buy things that didn't stamp a brand on your backside every time you sit on them,' Jo announced, fighting back.

Patrick looked taken aback. Then, unexpectedly, his lips twitched.

'I'm sorry you don't like my furniture. Perhaps you would be more comfortable somewhere else?' he suggested softly.

Jo managed not to flinch, but she read the ironic message he was giving her easily enough. He was going to send her away.

Well, she had always known that would happen if Crispin's brother came back. And her meeting with Patrick by the stream had in some obscure way made things worse. Infinitely worse.

She recognised the seeds of panic. She stamped on them ruthlessly and summoned up a cheeky grin. She even managed a shrug.

'Okay. Do you want me to go today?'

'You're not going anywhere until you've told me the truth,' he said with quiet menace. 'Then I'll think about what I do with you.'

So he was still thinking of handing her over to the police! Jo bit her lip.

'What do you want to know?' she asked warily.

For a moment he seemed almost at a loss.

Then he said, 'You can start with where you met Crispin.'

Well, that was easy enough. She shrugged again.

'In Lacombe. I told you. He got the Rolls-Royce wedged.'

'And you turned it on a sixpence and roared into the stockyard?' Patrick supplied, marvelling.

Jo flushed at the sarcasm. Her chin lifted.

'If that's how you want to put it, yes.'

'How convenient.' He was watching her narrowly. 'How much did you bribe Renard to quit? Or did Crispin pick up the tab?'

Jo stared. 'Bribe—? Oh, you're paranoid. That's crazy. Why on earth should I?' Her voice rose.

'Because your main aim was to get into my house and clear out the opposition,' Patrick Burns said flatly. 'You might as well admit it. It is perfectly obvious. My only question is, why?'

Jo was suddenly angry. It was a relief. She came off the embroidered seat in a bound and stood in front of him, her fists clenched by her sides.

'You're a nutcase. You know that? I didn't know anything about you or your house until I met Crispin. Yes, I was looking for a job. But that isn't a crime, is it? I was doing the rounds of the cafés in Lacombe—waiting tables, helping in the kitchen, anything.'

He looked down at her, unspeaking, unsmiling. She could not tell what he was thinking. Jo thought with sudden unease that she had not realised how very tall he was. Even when they were so close that she could see his warm chest rising and falling, his height had not been so obvious, somehow. Jo's coltish legs had always made her the tallest girl in the class. To feel suddenly small intimidated her.

It was a new experience for her. Jo did not like it. She flung her head back and glared.

'I wish I *had* got a waitress job. Anything would be better than this.'

His eyebrows rose in gentle incredulity. 'You'd better tell me why you needed a job.'

It was quite possible, Jo found, to fancy the pants off someone and still loathe them. She looked at him with dislike.

That too was a relief. Dislike was a lot better than that awful sentimental hunger she had felt by the river. Hell, she had even felt wistful about running away from him. Dislike was *heaps* better.

'People do,' she snapped. 'It helps them eat.'

He was not offended. If anything, he looked amused suddenly.

'How much of the stuff you told me by the river was true?'

Jo was tempted to say, *Everything; including the way my body responds to yours.* Of course she didn't. She had to tell him the truth, but only as much of the truth as she could bear.

His voice softened suddenly. 'Are you sure you're not a student, after all? Overspent on your grant and daren't go home. Is that it?'

Home! Jo could have laughed aloud. The only reason she had ever told a lie at all was to make sure that neither she nor Mark went within ten miles of Brian and Carol Grey and their cruel house, ever again.

She did not laugh. 'No.' Her voice sounded stilted, even to herself. 'I'm not a student.'

His eyes narrowed.

Oh, Lord, she thought, he had seen that moment of near amusement. His eyes were like lasers. She swallowed. She withstood his look, steady-eyed. But it was an effort.

'Of course you're not,' he said at last, softly. 'Much too sure of yourself.'

She did laugh at that—a great gulp of astonished hilarity. 'Sure of myself? *Me?*'

'You dealt with me very professionally by the river,' pointed out Patrick in a still voice.

Jo snorted in derision. 'No, I didn't. I *ran*,' she said, disgusted with herself.

There was a strange pause that she did not understand. Then he said, 'Yes, you did, didn't you?' in a voice she did not understand.

She did not understand the look in those tiger's eyes, either. She looked away.

'Right,' said Patrick Burns, as if he was having to wrench his thoughts back to the matter in hand. 'Stop playing games. You're not a student. But somehow you managed to pick up Crispin. And convince him that it was okay to move you in with a priceless collection of cars and a couple of elderly disabled people. Want to tell me how you did that? Or shall I guess?'

Light dawned on Jo. 'You think I'm a burglar?'

'Nothing so crude,' Patrick said. 'Let us say that I am toying with the idea that you might be the—er—advance party.'

Jo stared at him in blank incomprehension.

'You see,' he said conversationally, 'I keep remembering that you mentioned a boyfriend staying round here somewhere. And I ask myself—why didn't he keep you with him?'

Jo felt as if she had been frozen to the spot. She could not think of a single thing to say. His eyes bored into hers as if he could read her mind like an old floppy disk. She put up a hand, as if to shield herself from that laser analysis.

Then, to her astonishment, after a narrow-eyed moment he made a small gesture of repudiation.

'Maybe I'm wrong. If so, I apologise.'

It did not sound very apologetic. But it was something.

Jo pulled herself together with an effort. 'You can't have looked in your desk,' she said distractedly. 'Crispin took a character reference. I had to tell him to,' she added in self-justification.

Crispin had moaned about having to sit down and write to Jacques Sauveterre, but Jo had insisted. She had not known about the antique furniture in the house, but she had recognised the value of the veteran cars at once.

He looked sardonic. 'That was why I thought it must be a put-up job. I knew Crispin would never think of it himself. And a burglar capable of planning to put someone inside the target would obviously have thought of providing suitable references.'

'Oh,' said Jo. She was nonplussed. 'I didn't think of that,' she admitted candidly.

One dark eyebrow flicked up. 'No, I can see you didn't.' And lightly, with no change in tone at all, he said casually, 'Is Jacques Sauveterre your lover?'

She could not believe that he had said it. 'My *what*?'

'Or whatever you want to call it. Your partner? Your main squeeze? Your shag of the moment?'

Jo blinked. He sounded almost savage. She found she could not answer, could not think, could not *breathe*.

Their eyes locked.

After a moment he expelled an explosive breath. 'Okay,' he said in a more restrained voice. 'I think I accept that you're not here to steal my cars.' He paused. 'So what *are* you here for?'

She shook her head, still breathless. 'I've told you. I needed a job. By chance there was one here. It's nothing more sinister than that.'

'So why,' asked Patrick Burns lightly, as if he didn't give a damn about the answer, 'did Crispin tell you to pretend to be a boy?' His eyes sharpened suddenly. 'I take it that he didn't think you were a boy, too? Even Crispin couldn't be that blind.'

Jo flushed.

'He said you wouldn't allow a girl to work for you,' she muttered. 'Or to live here. He said you needn't know. That you wouldn't be back until I'd gone.'

'I—see.'

She sent him a slightly scornful look. 'It sounded daft to me. But it really worried Crispin. He said it was enough to torpedo the whole idea. Then, when I met Mrs Morrison and she thought I was a boy, Crispin said that was the answer.'

'It didn't worry you? Taking advantage of someone who is half-blind?'

Jo flushed even harder. There was a pause. 'I didn't like it,' she said at last, in a low voice. 'But—'

He flung up a weary hand. 'I know. I know. You wanted a job. And, as you've pointed out, it's a job you do well.'

There was something in his voice that suddenly made her think that it might be possible to stay after all. That he might be willing for her to keep the job—though no doubt on conditions.

But what conditions? She thought of that warm, naked skin. His eyes. The husky note in his voice when he had said, so intently, 'Where are you staying?'

A little tremor ran up her spine. The conditions might be impossible. Or more possible than she wanted to think about. And that was a shock. Gargoyles with big feet ought not to let themselves think thoughts like that. She didn't, normally.

Jo held her breath, not daring to meet his eyes.

'I still need someone to do something about the cars,' he said, almost to himself. 'Your records look as if you're pretty clued up. And you can always call for help if something is beyond you.'

He looked her up and down. This time, Jo could not read his expression at all.

'But—you?' he mused, as if he could hardly believe that he was saying it.

She knew it would be fatal to try and persuade him. But there was that room of her own, and all this wonderful landscape. So she said hardily, 'Why not me, if I can do the job?'

'It would be like importing a time bomb.'

Jo stared.

Patrick's eyes glinted. 'Well, would *you* say our first meeting was ideal for employer and prospective employee?'

Jo winced before she could stop herself. She remembered—and her heart did a double somersault in her breast. The way he had gripped her hand when she gave him back his shirt! The strength of it still lingered on her fingers, as if she had pinched them in a vice. She gave a little shiver she could not have controlled to save her life.

She hoped Patrick Burns would not see it. But he was hawk-eyed.

'Exactly,' he said.

'B-but will we see each other? I mean,' she corrected herself quickly, 'would we? You're not going to be here. Crispin said you were not going to be back all summer.'

'Crispin was wrong,' he said shortly. 'My plans have changed. I shall be here.'

Jo bit her lip. 'I could keep out of your way,' she offered in a small, despairing voice.

'You could try.' There was a grim amusement in his voice. 'Do you think you could bring it off?'

She frowned. 'It shouldn't be difficult. I never meant to come into the main house anyway. But the Morrisons were so friendly—'

His eyes glinted. 'I'm not—friendly.'

'No,' she agreed with feeling.

'Do you think that will make it easier to keep out of my way?' he mocked.

She swallowed. 'I—I suppose so.'

'Get real!'

'I can just stay in the barn and you needn't even see me.'

'But we will both know you're there,' he pointed out softly.

Jo looked at him, wary and confused.

Just for a moment the strange eyes changed. She caught a glimpse of the warmth she had seen by the stream. Warmth, and more than warmth; curiosity, a fleeting anticipation, a recklessness she recognised in herself, too. Even a sort of awe, as if this was so unexpected it was unbelievable.

She stood very still.

And then he shifted, broke the contact, turned and walked to the window. He thrust his hands into the pockets of his dark trousers.

Without looking at her, he said, 'Do you know why I don't allow girls to work for me?'

Jo was so shaken by that moment and its abrupt termination that she could hardly find her voice. She shook her head. He looked round, impatiently.

'No,' she said in a croak. 'But—'

'Eight years ago, when I began to be something of a celebrity,' he said evenly, 'a girl of very much your age decided she would like to be a celebrity, too.'

Jo was hardly listening to his story. So he was a celebrity, she thought. What sort of celebrity? Why, oh, why had she never bothered to question Crispin about what his absent brother did for a living?

'She thought the best way—well, maybe not the best, but the quickest—was to attach herself to me. Preferably permanently. If not that, then as publicly as possible, however brief the encounter.'

His voice was quite without emotion. He might have been talking about someone else. Jo was puzzled.

'What happened?'

'She joined my staff as a researcher. She was too young, of course. Still only in her second year at college.'

'Oh,' said Jo, with foreboding. 'Like you thought I was?'

'Like you, yes. But I knew her father in Washington, and he asked me to give her a vacation job.'

'What did she do?'

He looked at her briefly. 'It's interesting that you think it was she who did something rather than me. You are right, of course.'

He withdrew his gaze to the immaculate lawns again.

'She made it plain that she was attracted to me. More than that, that she wanted an affair with me. I didn't take it seriously. I was very busy. I didn't really pay enough attention, I suppose. I told her it was an adolescent crush and forgot about the whole thing. Even eight years ago,' he added remotely, 'I was too old for college girls.'

Jo winced. She nearly said, *I'm not a college girl*, but then thought better of it. Patrick Burns was still too old for her. Not just in age. In all his experience of games that he knew the rules of and she didn't.

It was just as well he was taking the trouble to kill those embryo fantasies of hers. They would not have done her any good at all.

Instead, she said, 'You forgot, but she didn't?'

'Yes. One night we were in Washington. Not just the two of us, of course. The whole team. I was doing an all-night commentary. She told the others she had a date and went off about midnight.'

Suddenly, Jo could see what was coming. 'Oh, Lord.'

This time he did not look at her. 'It was about four when I got back to my room. I saw a couple of photographers in the corridor, but, hell, they could have been linking with Japan, Singapore—anything. I didn't particularly notice them. When I got into my room, Maddie, of course, was waiting for me. All curled up in bed. No clothes, but full make-up.'

His voice was not emotionless now. Jo could hear the anger.

'She was even watching television to keep her awake.' He was cynical. 'She claimed she'd been watching me, of course, but it looked more like a late-night movie to me.'

'Why did she need to be kept awake?' Jo asked.

If she were curled up naked in Patrick Burns's bed, waiting for him to come home, she wouldn't have any trouble in keeping awake, she thought involuntarily. And she wouldn't have been able to concentrate on a movie, either.

She had a strange sense of suffocation at the thought. She pushed it away from her. That image walking around in her subconscious was not going to do her any good at all.

'So she could make the position plain. Either I took up her generous offer or she cried rape,' he said brutally.

'*What?*'

'She wasn't joking, either. I lost my temper. I was tired, of course. I could probably have been kinder. Some of it may have been my fault. I asked myself that over and over again—and so did the lawyers. But the plain fact was that I told her to get her clothes on and get back to her own room. When she wouldn't, I hauled her out of bed, dressed her myself and shoved her out into the corridor. To a reception committee with cameras and notebooks poised for my on-the-spot comments.'

'She told them you'd raped her?' Jo said in horror.

'She didn't have to,' Patrick said dryly. 'She was in tears, with her clothes all over the place, and I was manhandling her out of my room at four in the morning. The photographs made me look brutal enough for anything.'

'What happened?'

He shrugged, turning away from the window. 'I lost my job. Her father threatened all sorts of violence. I didn't blame him. He was a nice guy.'

'Were you prosecuted?' Jo was appalled.

'No. The thing never really stood up. As my lawyers kept pointing out, the guys from the newspaper had no reason to be in that corridor unless they were waiting for something. The photographers even admitted as much. And there were plenty of witnesses that she had been chasing me.' He made a sudden grimace of distaste. 'It became a political thing as well, of course, because she had worked for me.'

'Political?'

'There is a keen market for how-my-boss-harassed-me articles. Maddie did quite well out of it, I'm told. Although she still swears revenge.'

Jo thought suddenly that she would not like to be in Maddie's shoes if she ever met Patrick Burns again.

'And, of course, there are people all over the States who think I did it and should have gone to jail. Including my old friend, her father.'

That had hurt. You could see it had hurt. Jo made a small move towards him. She curbed it immediately. Whoever might be permitted to offer him sympathy, Patrick Burns was not going to allow a young girl to touch him again ever.

She said, 'I'm sorry.'

'It was not a good time,' he agreed. 'For a while I thought my career was over. Then I got the job with Mercury News and hit the really big time. It's not just celebrity in the States now. I'm recognised in every city where they have satellite television. Statesmen ask my advice. Rock stars ask me to their parties.' He sounded deeply cynical.

'And what do the young girls do?' Jo asked quietly. Because that was the point of this, wasn't it? He was telling her she had to go, after all.

'The nice ones run like hell. They know my reputation, you see. It's there in every profile in every magazine. I counted once. It's been written up in twenty-three languages.'

She did not commiserate. This was too important. She was not quite sure why.

'Okay,' she said levelly. 'And what do the others do? The girls who aren't nice?'

'They run like hell, too. But in the opposite direction. They turn up as interpreters, chauffeurs, chambermaids… I thought I'd seen it all. But not one of them ever turned up pretending to be a boy before.'

Jo's spine flicked straight as steel. She said, 'I'll go tomorrow.'

There was a long pause. Then he said quietly, 'Do you know, I think you've convinced me?'

She was turning away. She looked over her shoulder 'What?'

'I find I'm believing that you're only interested in the cars. That you're not preparing a story on "My Night with Dracula".'

Jo shivered again. She could not help it.

He said, 'It might just work.'

She said nothing. But she didn't leave the room, either. She looked at him, half resigned, half hopeful. And she really did not know what she was hoping for.

'All right,' he said at last. 'We'll give it a try. You can stay. And God help both of us if I'm wrong.'

CHAPTER FOUR

BUT it came at a price, of course.

'You've got to tell Nanny Morrison that you're a girl.'

It was almost a relief. But, 'She'll think I'm a real bitch—deceiving her like that when she can't see properly.'

'You should have thought of that when you started it,' Patrick said unsympathetically. 'Serves you right.'

'I wish I'd never set eyes on your stupid brother or your stupid cars,' she raged.

'Confess or move on,' he said, unmoved.

At least she had no illusions, Jo thought sourly. Patrick Burns didn't give a damn if she stayed or went. That little flicker of awareness had all been in her own head. As far as he was concerned she was not only a gargoyle with big feet, she was a liar and a cheat as well.

'I'll confess.'

'You'd better. I'll check.'

'I'll just bet you will,' muttered Jo.

He had picked up some papers from the big mahogany desk, but he looked up at that, his eyes glinting.

'Count on it.' He gave a nod. It was clear Jo was dismissed. She went, grinding her teeth. But she knew what she had to do.

It was horribly difficult. She cornered Mrs Morrison in the kitchen and had the worst time getting the kind cook to stop offering her food and listen. She stood first on one leg, then the other, muttered inaudibly, and at last got it out.

'I'm sorry,' she finished. 'I never meant— It's just that when you made the mistake in the first place, Crispin said that it was heaven sent. He said if you knew I was a girl you'd write and tell Patrick.' It sounded lame, even in her own ears.

Mrs Morrison said nothing.

Jo went on desperately, 'So the job sort of depended on it. And I really need this job.'

Mrs Morrison patted her hand. 'Don't worry, my dear. I've needed a job, too, in my time.'

Jo felt worse and worse. 'I never thought what a horrid position it would put you in,' she said wretchedly. 'I've felt a pig. It's the one thing that's spoiled this place ever since I started here.'

Now, of course, there was arrogant Patrick Burns to spoil it. But she wasn't going into that now. 'I am so sorry.'

Mrs Morrison put an arm round her and gave her shoulders a quick squeeze. 'There, there. No need for a drama. We all make mistakes.'

'You,' said Jo shakily, 'must have been an absolutely fabulous nanny.'

She had to dive for the garage or she would have burst into tears on the spot.

George Morrison was more inclined to take offence than his wife. He did not ask Jo to wheel him to the river that evening, like he usually did. But his wife was just puzzled.

'Why on earth did Crispin think I'd mind a girl coming here to work in the first place?' she said that evening over a kitchen supper.

George was not talking. Jo could not really blame him.

She said, 'I—er—I don't think it was you he was worried about. It was arro—' She caught herself. 'He said his brother wouldn't have a girl in the place.'

'Patrick? But why on earth? He has plenty of ladies come to see him and they stay as long as they want. George always says he's a bit of a rake, in fact. Don't you, George?'

George's offence dissolved a bit.

'I expect it's that business of the Kaufman girl,' he said, interested. 'Got him drummed out of America, that did. If Mercury News hadn't headhunted him he would have been down the Labour Exchange.'

Jo was puzzled. 'Labour Exchange?'

'Job Centre is what you call it these days,' translated George, thawing a bit more.

'George follows all the economic stuff,' Mrs Morrison said, proudly. 'Patrick says he's a walking encyclopedia—doesn't he, George?' She stopped, shaking her head. 'But that business with Maddie Kaufman was ages ago,' she added comfortably. 'And you can't say Patrick took against women because of it. He's always out with one or the other. I see photographs in the magazines.'

'In London, maybe,' said the shrewder George. 'When he can send them home. Remember how he insisted that Mercury get him a male PA? I reckon he's not going to let any of them get their claws into him again.'

'You're exaggerating,' Mrs Morrison said calmly. 'Anyway, Madame Legrain comes here. Stays the night, too.'

Jo nearly jumped. Then she caught herself. Of course Patrick Burns would have a lover. He was sexy as hell. Rich, too. And clearly successful at whatever he did. That arrogance told its own story. There was bound to be someone for sexy, glamorous Patrick Burns.

George sent his wife a minatory look. 'Gossip does no one any good. Patrick has had more than his fair share of it, I'd say.'

Mrs Morrison was unrepentant. 'It isn't gossip to say he's got a girlfriend,' she said placidly. 'I expect they'll get married one day. People just don't seem to do things in the same order these days.'

Jo thought suddenly, This is for my benefit. Ouch.

Could she have betrayed what had happened by the river somehow? That zing of awareness? Double ouch.

Outwardly, she intensified her boredom signals.

'I suppose so,' she said, helping herself to more salad with concentration. 'All sounds a bit elderly for me.'

The housekeeper was convinced.

'Will you still be staying over in the barn? It's bleak for a lass.'

Jo, to whom the Spartan lines of the bedsitter over the garage were an undreamed-of luxury, laughed aloud.

'It's great. I love it. Patrick—er, Mr Burns—never said anything about moving.'

George and his wife exchanged glances.

'Oh, well then,' said Mrs Morrison, after an odd pause. 'I won't make up a room in the house just yet.'

Jo said goodbye, and left.

It was just as well the motherly housekeeper didn't know how her heart jumped and dived whenever she looked at Patrick Burns, she thought. How just the turn of his head made something under her breastbone clench hard with fierce longing.

'Remember Madame Legrain,' she told herself robustly. 'And what happened the last time you let yourself get wistful over a man. Jacques couldn't run fast enough. You *can't* let Patrick Burns get to you.'

But there was nothing wistful about the way her blood leaped when those tiger's eyes rested on her. Worse, she was almost certain that he knew it.

Okay, then. She was going to have to be very, very careful.

'I can do that,' she said aloud. Though for a moment she almost wondered if the job and the roof over her head were worth it.

The evening had nearly turned to full night as

she made her way across the raked gravel to the barn. The house cast a long shadow. It enfolded the vegetable garden, the overgrown herb garden, the tangle of nettles and meadow grasses at the very end of the garden before it touched the open fields. The air was still, except for the sound of a distant bird.

Gorgeous, thought Jo. Her mouth tilted as she remembered the grubby streets and crowded pizza parlours she had left behind. Yes, it was definitely worth it. She would just have to find a way to neutralise arrogant Patrick.

She gave a choke of laughter at the thought. Fat chance. Patrick was not the sort of man to let anyone neutralise him. Even on the strength of two meetings she knew that.

She was still chuckling at the thought when she realised the barn door was open. Alarmed, she felt for her keys. But they were still there, safe in the pocket of her jeans. And she was sure she had locked up properly before she went to the farm. So someone with a key must have opened the door.

Her heart looped down and up as if it were on a yo-yo.

Friend or foe? Stranger or someone she knew?

Jo remembered how bravely she had told Patrick that you had to turn and face the enemy.

Over-confidence, or what? She could have laughed aloud at her own naïveté. She had never felt this sort of fear before—half trepidation, half a sweet, tremulous excitement. With a strong lashing of embarrassment thrown in.

Who am I kidding? I'm ninety-eight per cent certain it's Patrick in there! And it scares me to death.

She straightened her shoulders and went inside, treading as softly as she knew how. After the hot twilit courtyard, the cool interior struck black. Jo blinked, staggered, and put out a hand to steady herself.

'Made your peace?' asked Patrick Burns's voice from the shadows.

She nearly screamed. Only years of learning to keep a lid on alarm stopped her. She swallowed hard and took hold of herself.

'Yes. She was very kind.'

Her eyes grew accustomed to the darkness. He was standing by the old Rolls-Royce, one foot on the running board.

'So you're forgiven?' The quiet voice was ironic.

'Mr Morrison hasn't made his mind up yet.'

'He'll come round.' He sounded equivocal, as if he wasn't entirely sure he wanted George Morrison to come round.

'I hope so.'

'Oh, I'm sure you'll charm him into forgiving you in time.' There was a faint edge to his voice. 'Now, show me your living quarters.'

Jo looked at him doubtfully.

'You mean the apartment upstairs?'

'From what I remember, "apartment" is a bit of an exaggeration,' he said dryly. 'It was an attic when I last saw it.'

'Oh, no, it's much better than that,' Jo assured him. 'Come and see.'

He took his foot off the running board and came round the gleaming car to her. He was limping slightly.

'You've been standing in one position too long,' Jo said, leading the way to the stairs at the end of the garage.

He stopped at the bottom and looked up them, frowning. Then he looked back at the main doors, as if gauging the distance.

'Oh, the limp,' he said absently. 'No, I brought that with me. Anyone who comes into the garage has access to the flat, don't they?'

Jo wanted to ask about his limp, but he was clearly not going to talk about it. So she shrugged and answered his question.

'I think that's the point,' she said dryly. 'If you

have someone living over the shop you want to be able to talk to them whenever you want to use one of the cars. I thought that was why you had the flat built in the first place. Keep the chauffeur on call?'

'I never thought about it,' Patrick said, frowning. 'You're probably right. My godfather would have thought it was ideal.'

'Your godfather?' echoed Jo, puzzled.

'I inherited the château from him last year. Along with the cars.' He patted the nose of the gleaming T73. 'He was quite an autocrat, my godfather. I guess he would have thought that the chauffeur could take care of himself.' He gave her a sudden rueful smile. 'Sorry about that.'

Jo led the way up the stairs. She looked back at him curiously. 'Why?'

He followed her up the stairs more slowly. The limp was pronounced. How could she have missed that this morning?

He was impatient. 'Well, you're not exactly a bruiser with a wrench in one hand and a fistful of soldering iron in the other, are you? And this place is just too easy to get into.'

She looked over shoulder and saw that his frown was blacker than ever.

'Hell, sue me for political incorrectness, if you

want. I should have thought harder about the implications of your accommodation.'

Jo bridled. 'What? Why?' she asked belligerently.

He gestured to the barn door at the bottom of the stairs. 'This place is hardly secure. And a woman on her own—and young—you're vulnerable. Unless you're a kick boxer, I suppose. And I'd guess that you aren't. But you *are* reckless.'

'Reckless? Me?' She was amazed. 'I'm never reckless.'

He was dry. 'Then you're even younger than I thought.'

They had got to the landing outside her room. She was on the point of opening the door, but at that she stopped and looked at him suspiciously.

'What do you mean?'

His eyes were full of irony. 'You need me to tell you that stripping to the buff and swimming in a river on your own is reckless?'

'*Oh.*'

Jo wished he hadn't said that. She had been working quite hard at not thinking about their first meeting.

'What if you had got into difficulties in the water? It's quite deep, and there are trailing weeds that get wound round you. Or say someone less—restrained—than I am had come along?'

Or less uninterested, thought Jo resentfully. And shocked herself rigid.

She didn't want this ironic powerhouse of a man to be interested in her. Did she?

Of course not. She didn't want *any* man to be interested in her. In fact, she wanted to stop this line of thought right now.

So she muttered, 'Sorry,' in the sulky teenager sort of voice that infuriated her.

It did the trick, anyway. Patrick Burns stopped looking ironic and superior. Instead, he looked harassed.

'I've never paid much attention to the barn before. But now I've taken you onto the payroll, I suppose I'm responsible.'

He had reached the top of the stairs. He stood in front of the front door that led into her living quarters and looked it up and down disparagingly. 'Hell, look at that. Anyone could get in here.'

Jo gave a choke of laughter. In comparison with what she was used to, the flat was a haven of security.

Patrick did not like her laughing, she could see that. Well, he would just have to live with it, she thought. He was her employer. She would do an honest day's work for an honest day's pay. But she wasn't going to turn herself inside out for him.

She shrugged and opened the door. It was too narrow to pass on the landing, so she went inside and turned to hold it open for him.

'Hold on,' he said. 'No lock?'

'There's a lock on the outside door to the whole barn.'

She released the door and walked into the long, bright room that stretched over half the garage. It was still warm from the day's sun. It smelled of the wild flowers she had put in a jam jar on the table.

Patrick did not look at her domain. He stayed where he was, inspecting the door with a faint frown between strongly marked brows.

'No separate lock?'

She shrugged again. 'What's the point? No one ever comes here.'

His eyes locked on hers. 'I've come here.'

For a moment the silence between them was like a physical thing. Fog, maybe, in which you couldn't see your way. Or a rushing wind that blew you off your feet. She could not hear, could not *think*. All she could do was look and look at him. Jo put a hand to her throat to ease her breathing.

Then Patrick straightened and came into the room. The door swung creakily behind him.

'I was right,' he said grimly. 'Reckless.'

Jo could not help herself. She let out a great sigh of relief.

'Think about it,' said Patrick in a hard voice. 'You may like to dress like a car mechanic. But you're a woman, and sexy with it. And you're all on your own out here. If you called for help, what hope do you think there is that anyone in the main house would hear you?'

Sexy? *Sexy?*

She gave a little shiver. She didn't like that. Nobody had ever made her shiver before. It made her feel vulnerable all over again.

Vulnerability was not an option, she reminded herself. She stuck her chin in the air.

'Why should I call for help?' Jo said scornfully. 'I can look after myself.'

'From what I saw at the river today, I would say there was a distinct question mark over that,' Patrick said dryly.

Jo froze where she stood. The door finally shut. The catch closed with a noise like a pistol shot. As if the sound had released her from an enchanter's spell, Jo turned to face him.

His eyebrow rose questioningly. Mockingly. Jo

glared. But she blushed as well. He pursed his lips, looking at her tranquilly. His mouth tilted a little as he saw the colour running under her tanned skin. It made her even more hot and bothered. His eyes gleamed with mockery.

'Admit it. I scared you witless by the river.'

It was horribly close to the truth. Jo strove for some of her old brave flippancy.

'You didn't scare me,' she said. 'If you'd had a long black cloak and pointed canines it might have been different, but—' she gave him a gamine grin '—it was daylight. The moon is way off full. Nothing to worry about.'

'Interesting,' he said politely. His eyelids dropped. His lashes were long and black. It must be the dramatic frame they provided which made those eyes so memorable, Jo was thinking, when they lifted suddenly and his eyes locked with hers. 'No doubt that is why you took off like a rocket in the middle of the conversation,' he said softly.

'Ah,' said Jo. She eyed him warily. 'Would you believe I'd just remembered I had to be somewhere?'

He looked pointedly at her scratched hands.

'The middle of a bramble bush?'

In spite of her rejection of vulnerability, Jo was a realist. She turned her hands over ruefully, pulling a face. 'Yes, I see what you mean,' she admitted. 'Okay, that one doesn't run. Well, then—'

'Please. No more excuses. You were scared,' he said dryly. He added unexpectedly, 'I don't blame you.'

Jo gritted her teeth. 'No, I wasn't. I don't know why I shot off like that.'

The long, curling lashes dropped again. 'Don't you?'

Jo frowned. Was she being teased?

She had been teased by the boys at school sometimes. But it had felt different. And it was so long ago. The years on the road had made her practical and self-reliant. But they had done absolutely nothing for her ability to flirt.

This man had worked out that she was an amateur and was making no secret of the fact. It had not taken any more than one botched retort and he had found her out like a chameleon that had lost the ability to change colour.

Annoyed, she said, almost to herself, 'Life must have got too easy.'

Patrick was startled. 'What?'

'Three months ago I wouldn't even have noticed,' she muttered irritably.

He gave a choke of laughter. 'Wouldn't have

noticed you were scared? Or wouldn't have noticed *me*?'

But it was not either of those two, and they both knew it.

Jo turned away, trying to hide her self-consciousness under irritability. Not a bad effort, either. Slightly overdone, but you couldn't have everything.

'You've got the wrong idea about me. I'm not a schoolgirl. I've taken care of myself for years. I've had to,' she flung at him.

'Then you shouldn't have,' he said calmly. 'I think you'd better tell me about this self-sufficiency of yours. When did you leave home?'

She stiffened. 'What business is it of yours?'

Although his voice was soft, it took on a deadly note she was coming to know.

'If—I stress *if*—I'm going to be your employer, I've got a right to know what I'm taking on,' he said with irony. 'Now, no more evasions, if you please. When did you leave home?'

He held all the cards. Jo's resistance collapsed.

'A long time ago. Years.'

'Years?' His eyebrows flew up. 'And you're only nineteen now?'

She was annoyed with herself. She had forgotten that she told him that.

'I was an early developer,' she said flippantly.

'Hmm.' He did not smile. 'So you ran away while you were still a minor? Why didn't your parents have you brought back?'

'Not parents,' corrected Jo swiftly. 'Foster parents, if you like. I called them aunt and uncle.'

'Ah.' The look he gave her was troubled. 'Even so—'

'They didn't find me. I'm good at hiding when I want to be.'

'You must be exceptionally good if you gave the police the slip.'

'They wouldn't have called the police,' said Jo with certainty. 'Easier to cut their losses.'

Patrick frowned even harder. 'Were you some sort of wild child? Into sex and drugs and rock and roll?'

It was so unexpected that Jo laughed aloud, a great blast of uninhibited mirth. 'Not even close,' she said, when she could speak.

His eyes glinted. 'Wilful, then. A must-have-her-own-way kind of gal?'

'Like your Maddie Kaufman, you mean?'

There was a small pause. 'I guess I do, at that.'

Her hazel eyes danced. She shook her head. 'Nope. Not guilty. Never made a pass at a man in my life.'

'Ne—' He broke off, his expression arrested. His eyebrows flew up. *'Never?'*

Jo did not like that. In fact, she could have kicked herself the moment that unwary confession popped out. Desperate to retrieve the position, she stuck her nose in the air and said, 'Never needed to.'

But from the way he laughed she could tell he didn't believe her. Blast, blast, blast.

'Okay. I'll buy it. You weren't a tearaway and you weren't a drama queen. So what on earth was the trouble with your parents?' Seeing her brows twitch together, he corrected himself at once. 'Foster parents. Sorry.'

Rather to her own surprise, Jo decided on the truth. Well, quite a lot of the truth. As long as she didn't mention Mark there was no risk, after all. She gave Patrick a level look.

'You have to understand that I am unwanted baggage. My mother farmed me out. My uncle—well, he calls himself my uncle, but there's no blood tie—is a drunk and a gambler who doesn't take disappointment well. When he loses he drinks. When he drinks he hits out. His wife thinks that's okay, as long as he hits someone else. I,' she said, shaking her head back and looking at him challengingly, 'don't.'

Patrick's face went blank with shock. Jo had seen that before when she told people. After it came either disbelief or disgust. It was not going to be nice if this man looked at her with disgust.

'He hit you?'

She shrugged. 'Yes.'

She bit her lip. Well, he might as well know the whole ugly story. Then she would not be on tenterhooks in case he found out from some other source.

'The first time—the first bad time—he cracked two of my ribs. They took me to the casualty department of the hospital eventually, because it hurt me to breathe. I took a copy of the notes the doctor wrote about me. The second time he tried it, I left. I haven't seen either of them since.'

He looked shaken.

'Have you still got the notes?'

She smiled bleakly. 'Oh, yes. They're my insurance policy.'

The tiger's eyes glinted. She thought, *He understands that.* It gave her an odd little rush of warmth, as if she had just discovered something they had in common.

But all he said was, 'Far-sighted of you.'

Jo hesitated briefly. Could she afford to tell Patrick about Mark as well? She was tempted.

But it didn't exactly put her in a good light. There was more than an element of kidnapping in the story. She was not sure at all that Patrick would belong to the school of ends justifying the means. He might even insist on Mark going back. She couldn't risk that.

So she said nothing.

Patrick said, with deceptive mildness, 'All alone, with a couple of broken ribs! So where did you go when you left?'

Jo shrugged again. 'I told you. On the road.'

'What?'

She realised that she had made him very angry. She said defensively, 'What else could I do? I couldn't go to friends. My uncle would have beaten them up. He was violent.'

'But how did you live?' It was controlled. He was shocked, she thought. And fiercely angry. But not, thank God, disgusted. Not yet, anyway.

'A couple of my friends gave me some money when I told them what had happened. I slept the first night in a railway station. Then I went to Manchester. After a couple of days I got a job waiting tables at a lorry drivers' café. They didn't pay your stamp or your tax; they just paid you out of petty cash. So the staff got paid off regularly before any bureaucrats could ask questions.

There are lots of places like that,' Jo said tolerantly. She gave another laugh. 'I used to thank God for them. I must have worked in most of them, one way and another. You last about three weeks if you're lucky. Sometimes it's only a couple of days.'

Patrick looked stunned.

'But––where did you live?'

'Here and there. I kept travelling. The odd hostel. There were a couple of squats that were nice. Friendly—you know what I mean? One, in London, was really rough. They used a lot of drugs. And the guy in charge was mad. I got out of there as soon as I could.'

'Dear God in heaven.'

'It wasn't bad,' Jo said. 'Cold sometimes. At least nobody busted my ribs for me again. And then I found a women's refuge and they helped me get back on my feet.'

He surveyed her. At least the mocking light had died out of his eyes, Jo saw with satisfaction.

'I see why you're not worried about taking care of yourself,' he said wryly.

Jo shook her head. 'I told you—experience puts a few years on the clock.'

The dark face twisted, as if he had somehow applied pressure to a wound he had forgotten.

But all he said was, 'Yes. I can see that.' He was silent for a moment. Then he said abruptly, 'I'm sorry if I offended you. When I was nagging about the safety of this place.'

Jo was surprised. She gave him a forgiving smile.

'You don't need to apologise. Just don't try treating me like some little darling just out of school with a teddy bear still on the end of her bed. It annoys me.'

The golden-brown eyes flickered.

'I can see it would,' he said at last, gravely. 'And if I gave you the impression that was how I meant to treat you, I'm sorry. You've won your right to independence harder than most of us.' He paused, clearly picking his words with care. 'But look at it from my point of view. I can't help feeling that I'm responsible for what happens to you while you're—on my property.'

She opened her mouth to object, but he flung up a hand to stop her.

'No, let me finish. You're my employee. You're out here on your own. The barn is a good ten minutes from the house. And you're sitting above several million euros' worth of vintage cars. You must see that I am concerned for your safety. Any reasonable man would be.'

Put like that, there was not much Jo could say.

Although she could not help feeling that she had been out-argued by a master, she could not actually find any flaw in his reasoning.

'So, what do you want to do?' she said. 'I don't want to come and stay in the main house,' she added warningly, remembering Mrs Morrison's veiled hints.

'No. I don't think that would be a good idea, either.'

He smiled down at her suddenly. When he smiled like that his eyes went tawny. It made Jo's mouth go dry. She remembered *The Furry Purry Tiger* again. The furry purry tiger always smiled lovingly into the eyes of animals it was going to eat. The tiger looked so golden and beautiful that the animals forgot their alarm and walked towards it to be eaten. All the time its victims were walking towards it, the tiger purred. A little, superstitious shiver ran up her spine.

She said slowly, 'Do you always get your own way?'

He raised his brows. 'Why?'

'You'll do whatever you want here, no matter what I say. Won't you?'

'It's my house,' he reminded her gently. 'I'm afraid I will.'

Patrick's house. Patrick's laws.

Something in his face made her back away. 'Then look round. See what you want. As it's yours, anyway.' Her voice bit.

'Don't spit at me,' he said, amused. 'That wasn't what I meant. And you know it. I don't want to invade your privacy. Can't you see I'm concerned for your safety?'

Jo's chin came up as if drawn by a magnet.

'Nobody has to worry about me.'

'Well, I'm going to,' Patrick said, suddenly exasperated. 'If you want to work for me that's the deal. Take it or leave it.'

Jo's chin came down fractionally.

'I thought that would do it,' he said under his breath.

'Very well, then. Do what you want.' She tried to sound dignified but only managed to sound like a thwarted child, she thought in disgust.

He smiled that warm, tempting smile at her, that looked so beguilingly like affection.

Careful, she told herself, startled by the intensity of her instinct to smile back.

'I will,' he said gently. 'But I will try not to get in your way.'

He walked round the room. The pine floor-boards were bare and unpolished. They thudded dully under his uneven steps. He was limping quite badly now, Jo saw.

He stooped to look out of one of the triangular windows. Jo had put another jam jar of wild flowers and grasses on the window-sill. He touched a finger to a poppy petal.

'You haven't got much in the way of home comforts, have you?' he remarked, looking round.

The furniture had clearly been discarded from the house. It was clear why. It was also clear that Patrick had never seen the stuff before and was not best pleased to see it here now.

'A sagging bed, a kitchen chair with the back missing and two jam jars full of weeds,' he said, dismissing them with contempt. 'I'm sure we can do better than that.'

'I don't want charity,' Jo said, dangerously.

'Ah, but we've already established that it's what I want that counts,' Patrick said calmly. 'Don't pout. This is nothing to do with you.' A smile crinkled up the corner of his eyes suddenly. 'You take what I give you and like it.'

Jo muttered disagreeably. But she did not actually oppose him. She wanted the job too much. And anyway, although a roof over her head was a luxury, a mattress that was not made of lumpy horsehair would be an acceptable addition to it. Though her pride would not allow her to admit it aloud.

He was turning over the few battered paperbacks she had picked up from the market. They were well-thumbed and showed evidence of their adventurous lives.

'Books?'

'I like them,' Jo said simply.

Patrick looked at the spines. 'A catholic taste.'

'I like stories with a world of their own,' said Jo, defensive. 'It's good to forget your own world sometimes, no matter what people say.'

He did not seem to despise her for it, as she'd half expected.

'How right you are,' he said with feeling. 'And these are your escape routes?'

'Oh, no,' said Jo. 'Escape routes are much more practical things. They are your contingency plans for when things get seriously bad. The books are for fun.'

He was looking at her with an expression she could not interpret.

'Did things get seriously bad often?'

Jo laughed. 'Often enough for me to know you always have to keep your exit route open.'

Patrick said again, abruptly, 'How right you

are.' Then, before she could answer, or register a protest, he said in a changed tone, 'Window locks, I think, and a double door into the garage. We'll padlock the main barn door, of course. Now, what about the old fire escape that used to be here?'

And they were back to bickering about his design improvements again.

He spent over an hour wandering around, testing beams above and boards below, turning on taps and tapping pipes. He did not write down a single thing, but it was evident that he was making some sort of list in his head. Jo did not doubt for a moment that he would remember everything he had decided. And do it, too.

In the end, he flung himself down on the sagging bed. It squealed under his weight.

He grimaced. 'Not very good for the ego, that. You'd think you were overweight every time you sat down. It must have worried Crispin. He's always agonising about whether he's put on too much weight to ride that horse of his. I'm surprised he didn't order you a replacement on the spot.'

Jo shook her head. 'Crispin didn't come up here.'

Patrick raised his eyebrows. 'No? Then who moved you in? Mrs Morrison? I know George can't have.'

She shook her head again. 'No one. There's been no need. All the stuff was here. Mrs Morrison let me have sheets and a few other things.'

'So I'm your first visitor,' Patrick said softly. 'I would have brought champagne if I'd known.'

She was startled, and a little uneasy.

'You're not a visitor. As you pointed out, it's your house. I'm the visitor if anyone is,' she said lightly, trying to make him laugh.

She did not succeed.

'While you are here,' Patrick said with emphasis, 'this is your home. You ask who you want into it. And no one comes without invitation.' And then he did laugh—at her expression. 'Not even me after tonight, I promise. Though you'll have to ask me back to get that champagne.'

He stretched his leg a little, as if it was paining him.

'In the meantime, what do you offer evening visitors who have walked themselves off their feet?'

'There's lemon tea,' Jo said doubtfully. 'Or coffee. But it's only instant, I'm afraid. And no milk.'

'Lemon tea let it be.'

He watched her while she filled a small

saucepan with water in the galley area and put it on to boil. She was aware of it, and became all fingers and thumbs, nearly dropping the thick china mugs Mrs Morrison had lent her when she moved in. She made the infusion and brought it over to him.

'Thank you.'

Patrick moved to take it and grimaced involuntarily with pain. Jo watched with concern as he hauled himself round into a more comfortable position, propped up against the iron bedstead, his leg stretched out in front of him on the bed.

'How did you hurt yourself?' she asked, taking her own mug and sitting on the floor propped against the wall.

He looked surprised. 'Don't you know?'

Jo sniffed. 'Until today, I didn't think I needed to know one thing about you.'

Patrick laughed, his eyes dancing in spite of the lines of pain round his mouth.

'That's put you in your place, Burns.'

She did not apologise.

He said, excusing himself, 'I'm not all vanity. You see, so many people come up to me in the street because they know me, I forget there are places and people who don't.'

Because they knew him? Who *was* he, for heaven's sake? She would not ask. She *would not*.

'Then I'm doing you a double service,' Jo returned smartly.

One eyebrow flicked up in quick comprehension. 'Not only looking after my cars but also cutting my ego down to size?'

'Yes.'

'Remind me to be grateful,' he murmured.

'It will be very good for you,' she said with conviction. 'Are you going to tell me how you hurt yourself? Or is it my assignment for the week to look it up in the public library?'

He winced. 'I'm not that vain. It was very simple. I was reporting in a war zone and I got in the way of a sniper's fire.'

A reporter! So that was what he was. Now she knew what he did at Mercury Television. And now she knew why Maddie Kaufman had thought he was a celebrity worth trapping. 'My Night with Dracula' indeed, thought Jo.

She was impressed, though she wasn't going to show it.

'Then shouldn't you be resting instead of climbing around barn roofs?'

'It was weeks ago,' he said dismissively.

It didn't look it.

'But it's taking a long time to heal?'

'I'm fine,' he said curtly. 'Just can't break into a sprint too often.'

He didn't like that, Jo saw. He tried to sound as if he didn't care, but the light tone could not quite disguise the smouldering frustration underneath.

'Does that matter?' she asked curiously.

'It's my job. I work in war zones.' A muscle worked in his jaw. He was still curt. 'Being able to run kind of goes with the territory.'

'I can see that.'

Suddenly, unexpectedly, he was grinning. 'It's no good keeping your exits open if you can't get to them. And fast.' He glinted a look down at her. 'I'd have thought you'd understand that.'

He was teasing her. Jo found, to her surprise, that she could tease him back.

'Yes, I do. So we have something in common, after all,' she said, in mock astonishment.

He smiled straight into her laughing eyes, a long golden look that set her quivering even before she had time to register what he was doing.

'Oh, we have a lot more in common than that,' he said. 'Wait and see.'

CHAPTER FIVE

AT ONCE alarm flared. *Careful*, that inner voice said urgently.

Jo looked down into her mug of lemon tea until her eyes ached.

She knew Patrick did not take his eyes off her face all the time. She felt agonisingly uncertain of herself, of him, of the whole situation. Jo was not used to feeling uncertain. It was horrible. Her brows twitched together fiercely.

'You look very fierce,' Patrick said, amused. 'Have I offended you?'

Jo did not look at him. 'I don't understand you,' she muttered.

'Don't you?' It was gently mocking.

Jo blushed harder than ever. She could feel her long legs trembling, stretched out before her. Her whole body felt hot.

'No.' She decided candour was best and met his eyes, half reproachful, half defiant. 'You said you didn't want me here. You sounded as if you meant it. I thought you were going to kick me out. You talk as if you still might. And yet, here you are—' She broke off in confusion.

'Sitting on your bed and drinking your tea. Without so much as an invitation, either,' he teased.

She made an abrupt, half-angry gesture.

'That's nonsense. It's your house.'

There was a little silence. Then he said levelly, 'I told you. As long as you're here, this is your space.'

Jo shook her head violently. That was a trap she knew she must not fall into. Get too attached to places, and people, and you broke your heart when you had to leave them.

'No,' she said with determination. 'I have no place.'

He shifted sharply. She heard the bed creak and looked up. She was shocked by the look of agony on his face. She forgot her resentment as if it had never been. She forgot that her legs were trembling and that there was a strange sweet turbulence inside her whenever he spoke. She even forgot to be wary.

'You are in pain,' she said, her voice gentling.

He shrugged, looking annoyed. 'It's nothing.'

But Jo did not think it was nothing when it

could drain all the blood from his face, leaving the bones stark against the tanned skin.

'Have you seen a doctor?'

'It's in the diary,' he said indifferently.

'Have you got any medication for the pain? Can I get it for you?' she said in quick concern.

'Don't fuss. I'm perfectly all right.'

He was so sharp that Jo jumped. Her eyes snapped. 'Well, excuse me for breathing.'

He tightened his mouth, displeased. Jo glared right back at him.

After a moment, he said curtly, 'It's nothing. My leg stiffens up when I drive. I may have done too much today.'

'You mean you weren't sensible. So now you take it out on other people?'

His eyebrows flew up. 'I don't like to be reminded, I admit.'

'You get spitting mad,' Jo corrected dispassionately. 'And nasty with it.'

'Do you think I owe you an apology?' There was more than a hint of unholy laughter in his voice.

Jo was not going to let it beguile her. She stuck her chin in the air. 'At the least. And not for the first time.'

He laughed aloud at that.

'Again,' he agreed, his mouth twitching. He put

his mug down on the floor and began to rise with an effort. 'I'd better go, before I put myself beyond the pale.'

'Leaving me without my apology,' Jo said in a resigned voice. 'Why am I not surprised?' She stuck her hands in the pockets of her jeans and fixed him with an evil look. It was a challenge.

He limped to the door. Then turned.

'Don't look like that. I apologise. I apologise. Hell, I said you could stay, didn't I?'

Jo was implacable. 'And you'll let someone else do the driving tomorrow?'

But he did not find that so amusing. 'Take some advice, kid. Quit while you're ahead.'

Jo said nothing, looking mulish.

'You're very young, aren't you?' he said, almost to himself.

For some reason she did not contradict him. Normally she would have retorted that you grew up fast on the road, that she was more mature that people double her age. But for some reason, in the soft twilight of her attic, alone with Patrick Burns, she was silent.

He gave a sigh, unexpectedly harsh. 'So was I, once. Thought I could change the world. Long ago, Jo. Too long ago.' He held out a hand. 'Come here?'

Without a thought, without any of her usual alert wariness, she went to him. She put her grubby paw in his. He looked down at their clasped hands. His was immaculately kept, long-fingered, strong; hers delicately shaped but dirty and covered with scratches. He ran a thumb along one of the shallow tears, beaded with blood.

'You've torn the skin. I'll have to take care not to drive you into a bramble bush again,' he mused.

Jo remembered. She shivered, involuntarily. He felt the tremor in their fingers' ends.

'You must take more care of yourself,' he said softly.

And raised her dirty little hand to his lips.

Jo felt herself go scarlet. She jumped and pulled her hand away, furious with herself.

Patrick's eyes darkened. He bent towards her. Something very vulnerable began to beat high and hard in Jo's throat. She didn't like it. Vulnerability was very bad news; the worst.

'Don't,' she said in a strangled voice.

For a moment he looked as if he was going to argue. Then he shrugged and straightened, letting it go.

'You're right. I should go.' He looked at his watch. 'Mrs Morrison will have dinner ready, and I have calls to make before I eat.'

Jo nodded hard, a little too quickly.

'Good night,' she said. It sounded muffled.

Patrick opened the door and went out onto the staircase. He looked back, hesitating.

'Will you be all right?' he asked her with a searching look.

Jo found it easier to breathe once he was outside the door.

She said, with irony, 'I have been up to now. It's been very peaceful.'

His smile was wry. 'Then you shall have your peace back.'

He limped down the stairs without another word.

Jo went out onto the staircase to watch him go. She felt as if she wanted to call him back. Yet it was a relief of sorts when he was gone. But, then again, he left a void…

What is happening to me? thought Jo. *I don't do nonsense like this!*

At the foot of the stairs, he turned and looked up at her.

'I meant it, you know. You will be quite safe here. Safe and…' he hesitated '…undisturbed.'

She met his eyes. There was a message there. Jo nodded slowly.

She felt impatient with herself. It was not that she

was inexperienced, exactly. Her instincts had led her safely through years of living among vagrants, the bewildered and the dispossessed, and she trusted her judgement with people like that.

But with Patrick Burns she was in new territory. He had a quick, subtle mind. Worse, his sense of power was so innate that he was almost unaware of it. She knew nothing about men like that, Jo thought.

So—did she want to?

Because she could. That was clear. If she invited him back.

Was she going to invite him back?

He saw her hesitation. 'I won't invade again,' he said deliberately.

Jo swallowed, her chin lifting instinctively.

Patrick's mouth twisted.

'Your territory. You must have some decent locks, I insist on that. But you'll keep the keys,' he promised. 'I won't set foot over the threshold again.' His eyes were very steady. 'Until you ask me.'

It was such an accurate echo of what she had been thinking that Jo jumped. Was he a mind-reader?

Patrick misinterpreted. 'Not very flattering,' he murmured. 'You might, though. You never know.'

Jo's face shuttered. There was a moment's tense silence. Then Patrick gave an odd laugh and a quick, graceful shrug.

'No, maybe you're right,' he said lightly. 'Anyway, your choice from now on.'

He gave her a nod and limped across the garage and out into the evening shadows.

Jo went slowly back into her sanctum. She closed the door and leaned her back against it. She felt as if she had just been interrogated by an expert and wasn't quite sure what she'd given away.

He had been concerned for her *safety,* she reminded herself. He had not threatened her. Hell, he had been a whole lot more scary in the study, when he'd first recognised her. So why did the bedsit feel suddenly dangerous?

It was as if it had been her secret lair and wasn't secret any more.

The room was hot after the stifling heat of the day. Jo had left the windows shut against the sun, but the air was redolent of the summer in the meadows beyond. She recognised it. But there was another scent, too, now—a new one she did not recognise. Jo sniffed, wandering round the room. It was strongest by the bed, a complicated cocktail of starched linen and aromatic herbs and brandy. It was the last, sharp and expensive, that made her realise at last what it was.

Oh, yes, her secret lair had been well and truly invaded. Would it ever feel hers again?

She went to bed among pillows that smelled of Patrick Burns's cologne. It did not make for peaceful dreams.

Patrick limped back to the château. The stars were brilliant in the June sky, but he did not look at them. He was furious.

What an idiot he was. The girl had looked terrified.

He caught himself. No, not terrified. On reflection, he didn't think a lot terrified Jo Almond. But there was no doubt that she had wanted him gone just now. She had gone still, like an animal scenting danger. He hated the thought that he had done that to her.

His own fault, of course. He should never have kissed her hand. What on earth had possessed him?

He kicked the pedestal of an ornamental urn and staggered crazily. Double damn! He just couldn't get used to the way this leg kept letting him down.

Not just his leg, he thought with harsh self-mockery. As far as Jo Almond was concerned his judgement seemed to have taken a holiday, too.

One moment she's standing up to me, challenging me, even *laughing* at me, blast her cheek. The next I can't get near her.

I must be out of practice, he told himself, trying hard to be amused. But he could not quite banish the thought, darkly unwelcome, that followed it. Or I'm too old for her.

Jo slept badly. Having tossed and turned through most of the hot night, she'd fallen asleep eventually in the small hours and woken up with the sheet tangled on the floor and the pillows grasped to her like a lover. She lay there, hot and tangled, and thought: this is a new one. Wow!

She slid her long legs out of bed and padded over the floorboards to the window. The garden was deserted. It was too inviting to ignore.

She dressed quickly and went outside.

Birds trilled, but it was still too early for butterflies. When she walked on the grassy paths of the overgrown pleasaunce, her feet left footprints. The ornamental hedges were full of cobwebs, with the dew spangled along their threads like fairground illuminations. Drops of dew trembled on the edge of rose petals, just opening to the morning sun. The air was hazy with the promise of heat, but she could taste the early-morning breeze like the fizz of champagne on her tongue.

Jo drew a long, luxurious breath of delight—and stopped abruptly as a tall figure detached itself from the deep shade of a trellis of scarlet roses.

'Good morning,' said a cool voice, just on this side of mockery. 'You, too huh?'

Jo squinted at Patrick Burns. 'What?'

'Another one who couldn't sleep,' he elucidated.

Jo looked at him warily. 'It was hot last night.'

His lips twitched. 'Was it?'

'Yes.' Her tone said, *Don't mess with me.*

He took the hint. 'I thought it was because I did too much driving yesterday,' he informed her blandly. 'But you think it was just the temperature?'

Jo thought of that evocative scent on her pillows and could have killed him.

'Yes,' she said, her eyes daring him to dispute it further.

His eyes danced. 'If you say so,' he murmured.

'And it will be another scorching day today, too,' she flung at him.

'I'm sure you're right. Speaking of which—time you got yourself some summer clothes.' He fished in his pocket and brought out an envelope. He held it out to her.

Jo looked at the envelope as if it were a sleeping scorpion. 'What's that?'

'Money.'

'If you've got money to spend,' said Jo waspishly, 'you should do something about this poor garden. It's straight out of a history book and you're letting it be eaten alive by weeds. George and I do what we can, but it needs some proper loving care.'

'Don't we all?' said Patrick ironically. 'And your wardrobe, more than most. Take the money.'

'I don't want your money.'

He raised his eyebrows. 'And that should matter to me—why?'

Jo ground her teeth. 'I know,' she said ironically. 'Patrick's house. Patrick's law.'

That startled him. 'What?'

'That's what Crispin says,' she told him with satisfaction.

He chuckled. 'I like my own way,' he admitted shamelessly.

'I'll just bet you get it, too,' said Jo, displeased.

'Well, usually. But then I'm usually right.'

He met her furious eyes and laughed gently.

'Okay, okay. I won't tease any more. But take the money. After all, employers usually pay change-of-location costs. And that often in-cludes a suitable wardrobe.'

She thought of rainy Manchester and her an-noyance dissolved. 'You have a point,' she admitted ruefully. 'We left in a hailstorm.'

'There you are, then.'

'But—'

'But nothing.' Patrick looked at her curiously. 'Besides—wouldn't you *like* some pretty clothes for a change? Something summery?'

Jo knew what 'summery' meant. Lots of skin showing. She suddenly thought of blond and gorgeous Anne Marie, with her perfect legs and her sun-kissed skin. Five-foot-three blondes could wear cut-away tee shirts and floaty skirts even when heavily pregnant. Gargoyles with big shoulders and bigger feet ought to keep them-selves covered up.

She looked at him holding out the envelope. Smiling. Sure she was going to do whatever he told her to because she just couldn't resist.

It was too much.

'No,' she yelled.

She struck his hand away. And ran.

It did not end there, of course. After a couple of hours of car-cleaning therapy the Bugatti gleamed, and she went over to the kitchen for her usual morning coffee. And there was the envelope, in the middle of the big pine table.

'Patrick left that for you,' said Mrs Morrison unnecessarily. 'He said you need new clothes.'

Jo glowered. 'Dungarees suit me fine,' she muttered.

'Patrick doesn't think so.'

And that was the end of the matter. If Patrick wanted his garage mechanic to wear pink tulle and roses in her hair, Mrs Morrison would think he was quite right, thought Jo wrathfully.

'He said take the car and go to Lacombe. He wants you to buy a skirt and get your hair done. But be back by one. He has to go to Toulouse this afternoon and he wants to see you before he goes. He's ordered Luc from the village to drive him, for once. He said you insisted.' She beamed at Jo. 'You've done a great job there.'

Jo snarled.

Muttering, she went off to Lacombe and came back with the most severe skirt she could find. It was not designed for someone as tall as she was, and left too much leg bare. But there was nothing she could do about that.

The new hair was worse. The stylist had taken one horrified look at the nail-scissor cut and set about a major restructuring exercise. The result was a very short chestnut cap that gleamed.

Mrs Morrison was impressed when Jo went to the kitchen to report.

'I look—girly,' said Jo, making a face at herself in the mirror. She was half revolted, half fascinated.

'Well, you look less like a wild thing of the woods,' drawled Patrick, strolling into the kitchen unannounced. 'Oh, look—it's got ears!'

Jo went scarlet and wished that the floor would swallow her up. The Morrisons did not notice.

'She looks very pretty,' agreed Mrs Morrison. Adding, which didn't help at all, 'Don't you think?'

'Don't,' snapped Jo. 'It just encourages him.'

Patrick ignored that. He strolled over and took her chin in his long fingers, turning her head this way and that—as if, she thought, outraged, he was thinking of buying it.

'Very nice,' he decided.

She eyeballed him. 'Am I supposed to be flattered?'

Patrick met her eyes with deep appreciation. 'Not yet,' he said enigmatically.

Jo was deeply suspicious. 'Are you flirting with me?'

Patrick laughed gently. 'Trying to. Merely trying to.' And he turned her chin very gently, so that he could admire her profile. 'Is it working?'

George Morrison and his wife exchanged a startled look. Jo did not even notice.

She did notice that something was flittering about under her ribcage, as if her heart had come unmoored and started to doggy paddle.

She could have danced with rage. She shook her chin out of Patrick's grasp and stepped away from him.

'No, it isn't. Did you want me?' she said frostily.

Well, it was supposed to be frosty. But even before the words were out she heard how equivocal they were. Oh, God, how naïve could you be? She went scarlet to her newly revealed ears.

Patrick watched in deep appreciation. 'That depends,' he said suavely.

Behind him, George Morrison pursed his lips in a silent whistle and spun his wheelchair round.

'Better come and tell me which lettuce you want cut for supper,' he told his wife firmly. And, as she hesitated, watching Jo anxiously, *'Now.'*

Jo did not even hear them go.

'Depends on what?' she demanded, glowering and trying to ignore the heat in her face.

Patrick was bland. 'On how good your driving is.'

Jo stuck her nose in the air. 'If it's got wheels, I can drive it,' she said with total confidence.

'Then you shall drive me to Toulouse,' said Patrick in the congratulatory tones with which fairy godmothers said, *Yes Cinderella, you* shall *go to the ball.*

Jo was speechless.

The Mercedes was waiting on the sunlit gravel. The top was already down. She looked an aristocrat to her hubcaps. For a moment, Jo faltered.

Not so Patrick. 'Let's go, then.'

He slipped on sunglasses and then, to Jo's amazement, opened the driver's door for her as if she were a queen. She scrambled in, all legs and elbows, knocking a map to the floor. Patrick bent and handed her the car keys courteously.

For a moment she felt his breath against her cheek. Oh, there was that cologne again! The warmth of his body was as heady as the scent of the lavender fields she had walked past on her way from the village.

If she could have seen his eyes, would they have shown the same shock that she felt? But they were masked by the black lenses. Without the eyes, his face was an enigma. She could not guess what he was feeling. If he was feeling anything at all.

Patrick produced a battered panama hat and pulled it on before getting in beside her. He looked critically at her bare head. 'We must get you a hat.'

Jo decided not to argue. She had bigger things to worry about. She drew a deep breath and turned on the ignition.

She need not have worried. The car was a dream to drive. And Patrick, against the odds, turned out to be a dream of a passenger, too. He gave her clear directions on where to turn, but never once criticised her driving or caught his breath when he thought she should have braked.

When they pulled into the drive of a large mansion that announced itself as an orthopaedic therapy clinic, she congratulated him.

'Thank you. I do my best,' he murmured.

But Jo knew from the way one corner of his mouth turned up that he was teasing her again. Her mouth twitched in response.

She brought the car to a gentle halt in the car park behind the mansion. Handbrake on. Out of gear. Switch off engine. She turned to him, eyes gleaming.

'I did it!' she said, gleeful.

'You did indeed,' he agreed. 'Was there any doubt? I thought if it had wheels you could drive it?'

'Old bangers,' said Jo, waving a hand airily. 'Never a car like this. I'll confess now. I had a few butterflies.'

'Believe me, it didn't show.' He took off his sunglasses. His eyes were almost tender. 'You're something else, Jo Almond. Do you know that?'

She ducked her head then, laughing, not looking at him directly. But inside she felt warmed.

He sighed, as if he were reluctant to get out of the car. 'Oh, well. I'll be here for an hour or so.'

'What sort of therapy are you having?' He was so mellow, Jo reasoned, she could probably ask without getting her head bitten off.

She was right. He grimaced, but he did not crunch her.

'My London doctor recommended physiotherapy here. So I'm off to be stretched and pounded.'

'Good luck,' said Jo.

He got out. 'Town's that way,' he added, with meaning. 'They'll have a better selection of clothes than Lacombe, I imagine.'

Jo did not take the hint. Instead she wandered round, savouring the sunshine and having someone to meet later. It was like the sense of having a place and people to go home to when her day in town was over. This must be what being in a real family was like, she thought. Though it was odd to think of Patrick Burns as family. He was not brother or uncle material. She chuckled at the thought.

But it reminded her that it was two days since she called Mark. She went to a café and ordered iced coffee, then went to the public phone while the friendly waiter fetched it.

Mark was happy as a lark. He had learned to milk goats and he had gone swimming at the lake, where a local diving club had been practising. So he had had a try-out for it and they'd said he could be good. Jo had never heard him bubbling over like that. Tears of gratitude pricked her eyes.

Jacques came on the line. 'He is very well, Jo. We are all very well. But if he is serious about this diving we will need his guardian's permission. I think I had better call Madame Grey.'

Jo went cold. 'No!'

'But, Jo, he will have to talk to her sometime. Nobody will make him go back to that dreadful, drunken man. But his aunt…'

'She's worse,' said Jo fiercely.

Jacques sighed. 'Well, we can talk about this later. There is no hurry. When will we see you?'

'My boss has just come back from abroad. I don't know when my day off is yet. Jacques, promise me you won't talk to Carol.'

He hesitated. 'She should know that Mark is safe.'

'Promise me.'

'I will not call her until I see you,' he said. But his tone made it clear that he was not happy.

Her coffee tasted of sawdust. Then she lost her way when she left the café. She was late back.

Even so, Patrick was not ready. Monsieur Burns, said an elegant receptionist who disapproved of Jo's crumpled cotton, was still with Monsieur Lamartine. He was scheduled to stay in the clinic overnight, according to their records.

Shaken out of her preoccupation, Jo suppressed a grin.

'I think you'll find Mr Burns has other ideas.'

The disapproval turned to frost. Jo was given to understand that Monsieur Lamartine was second only to God. His instructions were ineffable, unchallengeable and guided only by the good of the patient. No one—*no one*—disobeyed them. Mr Burns, in fact, would do as he was told.

'I'll wait,' said Jo. She was beginning to have a fair idea of what Mr Burns would do in most circumstances.

So she was not surprised when in less than ten minutes a lift door swished open and Patrick, accompanied by two gesticulating people, limped out. His expression was one she knew. Jo deduced that he was being as awkward as he knew how.

She was aware of a sneaking pride in him, standing out against the full might of the Beverly Hills receptionist and the all-powerful Monsieur Lamartine. *That's my boy!*

'My dear Patrick, you are out of your mind,' she heard one of his companions say.

He was a neat man of medium height, with grey hair and a grey beard. From the receptionist's instant air of reverence, Jo concluded that this was the God-like Lamartine.

'I know what I'm doing.'

'You could delay your recovery,' his doctor told him with brutal frankness. 'Intensive physiotherapy, that's what you need. If you did your exercises it would be different. But you don't. Residential is much the best. I thought you wanted to get back to work?'

'I can work at home,' Patrick said. 'I can't

work here, with your staff busybodying around me all the time.'

'But they adore you!'

Patrick gave him a wry look. 'Quite.'

'You are an ungrateful devil and an unregenerate rake,' Monsieur Lamartine told him. But he was laughing. 'You shouldn't charm the hearts out of my nurses.'

Patrick shook his head. 'It's the charm of television,' he said. 'Nothing to do with me.'

Patrick's other companion now took a hand. It was a soft hand, with perfect painted nails, almond-shaped and lacquered to the colour of bronze.

'Patrick, darling, do you think you are being very sensible?' she said in a husky voice.

Jo went very still. Patrick *darling*?

She saw a tall, beautiful woman, with a cloud of pure Titian hair and a creamy skin that seemed younger than the worldly expression round her eyes. She was dressed in a simple black dress piped with amber. Jo did not know anything about clothes, but she realised with a little shock that the dress must be very expensive indeed. It looked like something out of a film. A very elegant film.

Jo, studying her first seriously groomed

woman up close, thought that she was a work of art. It must have taken hours to get that effect of flawless skin and wide-opened eyes. The cosmetics did not show, but Jo would have put money on there being several layers of them.

And this was the woman who called Patrick Burns *darling*? Jo suddenly felt very cold.

Patrick, however, was not showing any signs of major attraction. In fact, he was beginning to look strained.

'Don't start again, Isabelle,' he said wearily. 'I've got everything I need at the château.'

For the first time his eyes skimmed Jo's. She was almost certain that he winked. But he looked away so fast she could not be completely certain.

Isabelle said, 'I will drive you. I brought my car this morning especially. We can have someone pick the Mercedes up later.'

It sounded so intimate. Almost domestic. As if they had done this before. As if—Jo said it to herself deliberately, knowing she had to remember this—they were a couple.

Patrick looked as if he were going to explode. 'I'm not a complete idiot. I brought a driver with me.'

And he indicated Jo.

Two pairs of eyes turned in her direction. Two

faces expressed varying degrees of astonishment, doubt and displeasure.

Isabelle said, 'Darling, don't be absurd. You
can't let this child drive you anywhere.'

Patrick's mouth curled. 'Jo has joined the
residential staff,' he said blandly. 'She looks
after the cars.'

'The cars? Godfrey's beautiful vintage cars?'
Isabelle sounded horrified.

Monsieur Lamartine's eyebrows had
climbed, too. But now there was a look of
dawning amusement on his face. 'Unregenerate rake,' he repeated softly, on a note of
unholy amusement.

Patrick's face tightened. So too, more obviously, did Isabelle's.

'On the residential staff? You mean she's living
in the château?' This time, the elegant beauty
was more than horrified. She was angry.

Jo opened her mouth to explain about the barn.
She encountered a steely look from Patrick. She
shut her mouth again.

'I like having my staff on the premises,' he
said. He sent Jo a look of wicked complicity
which was not lost on either of his companions.
'It means they have no excuse for being late for
work.' His eyes met Jo's indignant ones and his

mouth tilted wickedly. 'They're even early. When they can't sleep.'

The private joke was pure mischief. And irresistible. Jo could not help herself. She chuckled.

Monsieur Lamartine's eyebrows hit his hairline. Isabelle frowned.

Isabelle said positively, 'I shall follow you. I would never forgive you if something went wrong.'

Patrick's smile glittered. It was not a very kind expression, Jo thought.

'Offering to change a tyre if it we get a flat, Isabelle?'

Jo did not chuckle again, although she could have done. The lovely lady's expression was eloquent. She planted herself firmly in front of Patrick.

'Darling—'

He kissed each scented cheek briskly.

'Very sweet of you to come. Quite unnecessary, of course. But sweet.'

Ouch, thought Jo. She was almost sorry for Isabelle, who didn't seem to recognise a put-down when it landed on her.

Isabelle put a hand on the lapel of his casual jacket. 'I will come out to the château,' she promised, gazing lingeringly into his eyes.

Patrick detached her hand and gave it back to her. 'Better ring first, to make sure somebody's home.'

If she were Isabelle, Jo thought, watching them dispassionately, she would take that for a definite brush-off. It would have crippled her with embarrassment.

Not Isabelle. She even blew him a kiss as he limped out to the car, leaning heavily on Jo's arm.

Jo was surprised. He had never leaned on her before. Was this for Isabelle's benefit? She helped him into the car and drove off.

As they swept round the front of the mansion, Isabelle was on the steps, watching for them. She fluttered her fingers in a playful farewell. Jo changed gear viciously.

'Don't say it,' Patrick advised.

Jo sniffed. 'You mean that you're a prat? Fine.'

It disconcerted him totally. 'What?'

'But I'm not supposed to say it. You can't take the truth, can you?' She was so annoyed with him she could have screamed.

'What are you talking about?'

'Only idiots have expensive physiotherapy and then don't do the exercises.' Jo kept her eyes on the road, her hands steady and her voice level. Even so, the repressed fury spilled out.

It sobered him. 'Oh, that. You may be right.

I thought you were going to take me to task over Isabelle.'

'What?'

'I heard the intake of breath,' he said dryly. 'You say a lot by not saying anything. All right. I could have been kinder.' Now they were on their own he had lost the insouciance. He sounded tense and tired. 'But nobody asked her to come to the clinic. I don't like people fussing over me.'

'I'd never have guessed.'

He gave a crack of laughter. Some of the tension evaporated. 'Trouble is, Isabelle doesn't tune in when people are telling her things she doesn't want to hear.'

'What doesn't she want to hear?'

Out of the corner of her eye, she saw his mouth thin.

'She fancies herself as the loyal sweetheart of the returning hero,' he said brutally. 'Specifically, me. She doesn't want to hear that it's not going to happen.'

Jo was shocked.

She did not say so. But it must have shown because he said, in a harsh voice, 'Yes, that's not the sort of thing a gentleman would say. Well, you might as well know. I'm many things. Gentleman isn't one of them.'

He tipped his head back against the cushioned headrest. She thought he closed his eyes.

He said, almost to himself, 'And I don't pretend to be. Ever.'

CHAPTER SIX

PATRICK looked at Jo sideways. God, she was pretty. That *skin*—

Her chestnut hair was riffled gently by the breeze. Suddenly the smooth sophisticated cut was gone and her head was covered with soft feathers like a newly hatched chick. His fingers itched to reach out and tuck a feathery frond behind her ear. She had beautiful ears, too, now he thought about it. He found himself thinking of Botticelli seashells. He wanted to touch the marvel of her ear, the soft vulnerable line of her jaw, the pugnacious chin.

What would she do if he did just that?

Probably drive them straight off the road into a row of vines!

Patrick had to admit it. His famous, irresistible sex appeal was simply not pulling this time. The ladies cloakroom would never believe it.

Good for me, he thought wryly.

But it didn't feel good for him. It felt—wrong.

Oh, boy, vanity has well and truly taken hold of you, Patrick Burns. You can't expect to attract every woman in the world, you know.

I don't want to attract every woman in the world. I just want to touch Jo Almond.

Touch?

Caress. Stroke. Kiss. Surprise. Make laugh. Make love to.

He drew a sharp breath and shifted in his seat.

Jo took her eyes off the country road for the briefest moment. 'Going too fast?'

He mocked himself silently. 'Not at all.'

'But you winced.'

He crossed one leg hastily over the other. 'Brief twinge. Nothing serious. You're very confident in a car, aren't you?'

'I told you I could drive anything,' she said, so proudly that he wanted to stop the car and kiss the life out of her right then.

'So you did,' he said on a ghost of a laugh. 'Where did you learn to drive?'

She smiled at the road ahead. 'School car park. Three lessons from the car maintenance teacher. Then hot-wiring teachers' cars on a Wednesday evening.'

He gave a crack of laughter. 'A tomboy with criminal tendencies?'

Her face shadowed. 'Suppose so.'

The trees met over the open top of the car. It brought a welcome breath of coolness. But she did not smile again.

He had hurt her feelings, Patrick thought, annoyed. How? Shouldn't he have said *criminal tendencies*? But he had already accused her of infiltrating his house to steal the cars, and it hadn't made her look like that.

Then he thought, I shouldn't have called her a tomboy! She had been pretending to be a boy for weeks. Maybe she was sensitive about it.

Probing, he said, 'Did you always love cars?'

Jo folded her lips together. 'No.'

He dug again. 'But you do now?'

She shrugged.

'So where did you learn about them?'

Not taking her eyes off the road, she said, 'At school. My aunt decided I had better learn a skill. She said I wasn't pretty enough to be a hairdresser.'

Her voice was very level. But Patrick was a journalist. He was a skilled listener. And when he listened to Jo Almond he engaged brain and gut and heart. He heard the repressed emotion churning as clearly as if there was a kettle drum on the soundtrack.

'What nonsense is this? Not *pretty* enough to be a hairdresser?'

Jo's hands tightened on the wheel. She was perfectly in control. Their speed did not flicker by a kilometre. But he saw her knuckles whiten. She did not answer.

Patrick wanted to hit someone. Instead, he said in a neutral voice, 'Did you *want* to be a hairdresser?'

The taut hands on the wheel relaxed. Jo's laugh was a pure shout of joy. 'Me?' She touched a hand to her newly gleaming cap, as if it were still the draggled mop he had seen in the river. 'You're joking, right?'

He did not answer that directly. 'What did you want to be, then?'

She glanced at him sideways. 'You'll laugh.'

'Try me,' he invited.

'I wanted to learn Latin,' she said curtly.

That really startled him. *'Latin?'*

'And history and foreign languages and drama and… Oh, lots of things. I always wanted to know stuff. Carol said there was no point in educating me above my station.' Her narrowed eyes did not augur well for Carol if their paths crossed again.

Aha, thought Patrick. 'Carol is your aunt?'

'That's what she liked us to call her,' Jo said coldly. 'She got paid.'

His eyebrows rose. 'She doesn't sound like a woman who should have had charge of children.'

Jo snorted. 'Too right. Not that she looked on herself as a carer, exactly. She said people paid her to take away their garbage,' Jo reported dispassionately. 'That was us. Rubbish our parents didn't want.'

Shocked, Patrick sat bolt upright.

Jo glanced at him again. 'I'm going too fast. That definitely jolted your leg.'

Patrick said impatiently, 'Considering what I paid for these springs you ought to be able to hit Mach One before my leg is jolted. How do you know your parents didn't want you?'

Jo shrugged. 'Why else would they unload me?'

'There could have been all sorts of reasons,' said Patrick the journalist, fascinated in spite of himself. 'Illness. Poverty. Some terrible personal problem. Have you ever spoken to them? Asked?'

She made a small negative movement. 'I don't know a thing about them.'

He digested that. 'Have you tried to trace them?'

'No.'

'I'm no expert, but I'm sure it could be done. You weren't adopted, right?'

Jo shuddered. 'No.'

'So you kept your original name?'

'Yes.'

'Anything else?'

They had turned off the main highway onto a little up and down road, with hedges close to both sides of the car. Jo took her eyes off the road long enough to cast him a pitying glance.

'You mean have I got a birthmark and a ring with a mysterious crest on it? Nope. I've got a birth certificate, father unknown, and a children's book.'

'Well, that's a start. I could probably help, if you wanted. I know researchers who would know where to go for advice.'

Jo said coolly, 'My mother got rid of me. When someone does that, I stay got rid of.'

Patrick studied her. Her skin was soft as apple blossom. But her expression was like iron.

He said gently, 'There's no need to look like that. No one can make you do anything you don't want to.'

She did not soften. 'I know.'

He raised his eyebrows. 'Wow. That's some confidence you've got there.'

'Sorry,' she said, not sounding it.

'Don't be. I like it.'

That disconcerted her at last. She sent him a doubtful look. 'You like confident people?'

Patrick said carefully, 'I like people who know their own minds.'

He watched her think about that.

'I'd say that sounds as if you have bullied a lot of people into changing their minds in your time,' she observed.

He sat upright, disconcerted.

'Bullied? Ouch!' He looked at her. 'You really don't think much of me, do you?'

'I don't think it would be easy to resist you once you'd made your mind up,' she said honestly.

'You managed it,' Patrick said in an idle voice.

'What?'

'Think about it.'

'I thought I'd rolled over and done everything you told me to,' Jo said, trying hard to keep the resentment out of her voice.

'Not from where I'm standing,' he said ruefully.

She frowned, not understanding.

'The first time we met?'

'The first time we met you told me to apologise to the Morrisons and I jumped to and did it.'

'Not the first,' he reminded her softly. 'By the river.'

Even then, it took her a few seconds to realise what he was talking about. When she did, she went crimson. For the first time the big car swerved.

He put out a hand and steadied the steering wheel. The long brown fingers were warm over her suddenly nerveless grip.

'That's—not fair,' she said breathlessly.

'No, I suppose not.' He sounded amused.

And he tightened his hand strongly over hers before he took it away.

She said in a high voice, 'You're right. You're not a gentleman.'

'I'm glad you remember that,' Patrick drawled.

But he wasn't. He was furious.

He didn't want to fence with Jo Almond. He didn't want her to try to play sophisticated games, throwing his own words back at him, keeping him at arm's length. He wanted to say, *Stop the car. Talk to me. Tell me you feel it, too.*

That was when she astounded him. She swallowed. Fascinated, he watched her throat move.

She said with difficulty, 'By the river—it was—you shocked me. I wasn't *prepared.*'

The honesty of it staggered him. For a moment he was utterly silenced.

Then he gave a soft laugh and said, 'What would you say if I told you that the shock was mutual?'

At once he thought, *I shouldn't have laughed. Why did I laugh? She'll think I'm laughing at her.*

This time Jo had herself and the car well under control. It did not deviate by a millimetre from its course along the straight stretch of leafy road.

She said carefully, 'I'd say it was very unlikely.'

Still castigating himself, he said almost at random, 'How do you make that out?'

'Shock,' Jo said levelly, 'means you've lost control. You don't.'

Yes, laughing had certainly been a big mistake. She was no fool, this odd, awkward, gorgeous girl. And she wasn't going to let him off the hook with the clever half truths that usually served him for flirtation.

'You told me that experience speeded up the clock,' he said at last, rueful. 'I should have remembered that. You're the strangest nineteen-year-old I've ever come across.'

She was watching the road and did not answer.

They were approaching a fork. She slowed the car. Patrick jerked himself out of his dark reverie.

'Left,' he said. 'Down the hill, bear right. Shortcut. With an added bonus.'

Jo nodded and set the great car easily down the narrow lane. In some places the track was so narrow that the bushes touched the edge of the car.

'Under the arch where the trees meet over the road, sharp left, and up a steep hill. Then draw in to the side of the road.'

'Why?' she said suspiciously.

Patrick bit back a smile. 'You'll see.'

He could feel her withdrawal. Oh, yes, she was no fool. She saw trouble on the horizon and braced herself. Suddenly he did not want her bracing herself against him.

He said roughly, 'Don't worry. I'm not going to make a move on you. It's just the perfect view of the château.'

She followed his instructions, taking the car at a crawl through the overgrown lane. They were climbing up and up. The road spiralled. Fronded branches of chestnut trees met over their heads. It was like climbing the tower of a cool green church.

And then suddenly they were at the top. There was a small parking place under the trees. Jo brought the Mercedes to rest and turned off the engine. The hillside fell away to the left of them, down to a small river valley. And on the hillside opposite was the château, walled and turreted in the evening sun. She had seen pictures like that, in books at school. But the pictures had all shown knights in armour and prancing horses, with ladies in tall conical hats and flowing gowns looking on.

'Oh,' said Jo on a long breath. 'Only there should be pennants flying.'

Patrick sat back, well pleased. 'We'll raise a standard the moment we get back this evening,' he promised.

'We—' She did a double take, looking at the exquisite scene again. 'You mean you're serious? That's *our* château? I mean your château?'

'That's our château,' he agreed softly. 'You shall fly your pennant over it just as soon as I can get you one.'

Jo didn't know how to respond to that. She cleared her throat noisily. 'I didn't realise there was a river on this side,' she said, in an unnaturally high voice.

Patrick stretched lazily. 'Same old river you were swimming in. It curves round the place, just further downstream. When we leave, we will go down the hill and over a seriously rustic bridge to reach the original entrance. The last time I visited it was overgrown with stinging nettles.

But at least that will prove to you that it is our château.'

They sat for some time in silence, watching the towers turn to gold as the sun got lower in the sky.

At last he stirred, and Jo set the car in motion again. As he'd said, the bridge over the small river was wooden. It creaked ominously as she whispered the Mercedes across it.

The gates on the other side were made of the same wrought-iron as those to the main drive, but they were smaller and not electronically programmed. She stopped the car and made to get out. Patrick forestalled her.

'I'll open them.'

He unlocked the gates with a small modern key from his keyring. Then he swung a big oval catch and pushed. The gates opened soundlessly.

Jo engaged gear and drove through. She stopped and looked back. The wooded hillside and the wooden bridge lay basking in the afternoon sun. Upstream, meadows lay like a rich brocade coverlet, shot with silver. Nothing moved in the humming heat.

Patrick closed the gates behind them and limped back to the car.

The sun was hot on her shoulders and bare arms. Jo could feel him looking at them. She swallowed.

'Come and sit in the shade,' he said softly.

Her breathing quickened. 'Surely—we—I mean—Mrs Morrison will want to know… they'll be expecting you…'

She wanted to go and sit in the shade of the willows with him. And she did not want to. She was afraid of it. She wanted to defy the fear. It seemed to be inviting her to take a step into a dimension she had never entered before. Where she might end up not knowing herself.

Patrick leaned on the car door and touched his hand against her cheek. Jo quivered. An electric shock would have been milder, she thought, shaken.

'You look hot,' he said softly. 'It will be cool by the river.'

She might look hot, thought Jo. But she was shivering. In fact, she was shivering so hard she was surprised he did not see it.

'Come along,' he said, in such a tender, serious voice that her eyes prickled with unexpected tears. She, who never cried!

And she, who never went into anything she wasn't certain she could get out of, said, 'Yes,' in a suffocated voice.

Patrick leaned into the car and switched off the engine. His arm nearly brushed her breast. So nearly, Jo felt as if she had forgotten how to breathe. Silently, he opened her door for her. Jo got out as if she were in a dream.

Keep your exit route open, she reminded herself feverishly. Keep your exit route open.

But what good were exit routes in a dream?

They walked to the bridge. He did not touch her, though she more than half expected it. She held herself tensely.

'Relax. I'm in no physical condition to throw you to the ground and ravish you.' There was an edge to Patrick's voice. 'Nothing to worry about here.'

She stuck her nose in the air. 'I'm not. And you'd never worry me, anyway. If I can't run I can always fight. And I fight dirty.'

Patrick flung back his head and roared so hard that he had to stop while he put his hand to his side, shaking with mirth.

'I'll just bet you do,' he said, when he could speak. No edge to his voice now. Just deep appreciation. 'Come on. There should be a seat here somewhere. I used to bring Tolkein down here.'

He forged his way through an undergrowth of hawthorn, hazel and weeds. Jo followed cautiously. But he always paused to hold back a trailing branch for her, or lift her over a place where small streams turned the undergrowth to mud.

'Very Tarzan,' said Jo, more breathless than her exertions really required.

'Aren't I just?' he said, setting her down, his eyes wicked.

They found the place he was looking for. It was an elderly tree, and at some time someone had placed a circular iron seat round its trunk. Two sections of this had rusted and collapsed, but one was still standing.

Patrick sat on it and straightened his injured leg out in front of him. Jo dropped onto the mossy riverbank beside him. The cascading branches at her back tangled in her short hair. She crossed her legs in front of her.

The water lapped peacefully against the bank under the shelter of the tree. There was a smell of sun-dried grasses and herbs.

Jo sighed with pleasure.

'This is a perfect place,' she murmured.

'Yes,' he agreed, detaching trailing willow fronds from her hair with an idle hand.

It was rather pleasant, Jo decided. Like being stroked.

'Tell me about your family?' she asked. 'I mean, is this your family home?'

'Specify family.'

She was puzzled. 'I'm sorry?'

'You really don't read the profiles, do you?' He sounded amused again. 'It's public knowledge. My mother is a political hostess by metier. She's been through four politicians of various potential since I was born.' He paused, then said reflectively, 'There was a time when I couldn't go into the Senate dining room in Washington without bumping into a couple of ex-stepfathers. Home was wherever the present one was campaigning.'

It was so far from everything Jo knew she could hardly imagine it. She said curiously, 'Wasn't that odd?'

'I didn't know it was odd,' Patrick pointed out, stretching his long legs in front of him and locking his linked hands behind his neck. He looked up through the leaves of the willow. 'I learned to travel light and take my treasures with me. That stood me in good stead as a foreign correspondent. I guess you could say the château is the first home I've ever had.'

'Why France?'

Patrick grimaced. 'My godfather took his responsibilities seriously. He said stepfathers could come and go but a godfather was for life. I used to holiday here with him a lot. When he died he left it to me.'

'Are you going to live here?'

He was suddenly serious. 'If you'd asked me six months ago I'd have said not a chance. I thought of turning it into an upmarket hotel. Conference centre with swimming pool thrown in. Golf course and horse riding on tap. You know the sort of thing.'

Jo didn't. But she could guess. It was a style of life that she had only read about in other people's discarded glossy magazines.

She looked at the water, half rueful, half sad. Nothing could have made it more obvious how far apart their worlds were. Patrick Burns was so used to that degree of luxury that he assumed everyone else would recognise it, too.

She did not reply. But her mouth twitched a little. Patrick saw it at once.

'No, stupid of me,' he said softly. 'Of course you don't.'

There it was again, that fast tuning in to her thoughts. It was unsettling.

She said quickly, 'What made you change your mind? About turning it into a hotel, I mean?'

There was a little pause, as if he was debating whether to answer her or to insist on pursuing his own line of interest. But in the end, he decided to answer.

'I'm not sure I have,' he said slowly. 'But— well, I might need a family home sometime soon.'

At once, like a snake striking, the thought hit her: Isabelle? Then—surely not? He said it wasn't going to happen.

That was a thought that Patrick did not tune in to notice, though. He was absorbed in his own line of thought. 'Everyone says I'm crazy.' He looked down at her broodingly. 'I wonder what your take would be?' he mused.

Jo hugged her knees. 'Try me,' she said dryly, as he had said to her.

He said, as if the decision surprised him, 'All right. I will. I want to adopt a child. What do you think of that?'

Jo's first reaction was a huge rush of relief. *Not Isabelle, then.* Then she actually thought about it. 'Adopt? Why? More important, who?'

'Ah,' he said with satisfaction. 'I was right about you. You ask the right questions. None of my clever lawyers did.'

'Thank you,' said Jo. 'I think. Does that mean I'm not clever or not a lawyer?'

He gave a crack of laughter. 'Don't fish for compliments. You're too sharp by half, that's what you are, as Nanny Morrison would say.'

Jo smiled. 'So, who is this child you want to adopt?'

'He's an orphan. He has no home, no family, and

damn little food. For the moment, he's living in a refugee centre in the mountains. He saved my life.'

'What happened?'

'I went to do an interview in a small town. It was a set-up. As soon as my cameraman and I arrived all the shoppers melted away and a couple of snipers opened up. I was sitting at a café in the middle of the square. I was a sitting duck.' It was chilling, the matter-of-fact way he said it.

Jo put her hand on his knee, as much to reassure herself that he was there, flesh and blood, as to offer comfort. His hand closed over hers, strongly.

'I flung myself to the ground, with my hands over the back of my neck. But I thought it was the end for me. Then this child—Pavli—just ran out from the shops and sat beside me. He was one of them, you see. A local. His parents had been killed in the bombardment only a few weeks before. None of the snipers was going to risk killing him. So he saved me.'

'What is he like?'

Patrick intertwined his fingers with hers, almost absently. 'Do you know, I'm not really sure? We communicate in bad French. Brave, of course. Very resourceful. He took charge of a bunch of refugees. I helped them get over the border. He's kind to people.' He looked down at their twined fingers. 'I owe him,' he said in a low voice.

'Yes,' said Jo, moved.

He looked up, suddenly eager. 'So you don't think I'm crazy, wanting to adopt him?'

Jo said carefully, 'I don't know. What does Pavli want?'

It shattered Patrick. 'I don't know. I never asked—I assumed.' He released her fingers and pushed his hand through his hair. 'Surely life would be better for him with me? The opportunities...' But she could see that he was struggling for his arguments.

She said gently, 'Why do you want him? Just because you owe him?'

Patrick stared at her. All the conflicting emotions were plain to read in his face.

'From my experience,' said Jo very softly, 'a child should go where he feels he has a place. All the rest is incidental.'

Patrick stared, as if he was concentrating his whole being on her words.

'Explain.'

'No one should be a charity case all their lives,' said Jo with feeling. 'Pavli has other people he has helped besides you. That makes them a sort of family of fellow sufferers. Are you going to adopt them all?'

'No,' he said, arrested.

She shrugged. It was more eloquent than words.

'I...*see*,' he said on a slow note of comprehension. 'Yes, I see. Oh, wise young judge!' He stirred. 'And where did you learn so much about people, Jo? From the boyfriend who got first claim on the place to stay?'

She almost jumped. She had forgotten that she had unwarily referred to Mark and he had inferred he was her boyfriend.

'No. Myself mainly. And my foster brother.'

He waited, but she didn't say anything else.

'You don't give a lot away, do you, Jo? Are you close, you and this brother?'

She hesitated, suddenly alert. She did not really believe Patrick would give them away if she told him about Mark. But it wasn't her secret alone.

'We don't see a lot of each other,' she said uncommunicatively.

'So you're solitary?' he remarked. 'Another thing we have in common.' And he leaned forward and smiled straight down into her wary eyes.

Jo froze.

'No ties,' he elaborated softly. 'No one close.

Relying only on ourselves. Keeping the rest of the world at arm's length.'

She could not tear her eyes away from his.

'Soul mates, one might almost say.' It was half mocking, half another one of his obscure challenges. 'I told you we had more in common than you thought.'

Jo felt her breathing quicken.

'I don't see that we're alike at all,' she said, too quickly and too loudly. 'You're rich. And famous.'

He was watching her quizzically. 'Am I?'

She glared. 'Well, aren't you? Everyone keeps telling me you are.'

His smile grew. 'But you've never heard of me,' he pointed out softly. 'I can't be that famous, can I?'

'That's got nothing to do with it. I don't see TV often—' She broke off, realising too late how neatly he had got that admission out of her. *'Oh!'*

She pressed her hands to her hot cheeks, hating him.

He stretched lazily. 'It's okay. I knew you'd never heard of me.'

Her blush subsided. But not her annoyance. She had been so careful to hide it! 'How?' she demanded, truculent.

He paused, considering. 'Something about the eyes, I think.'

'Oh, pu-lease.'

'Believe it. When you look at me, you see a stranger.'

Jo stared. 'So?'

'Most people don't,' he said simply. 'I've been in their living rooms too often.'

'Oh.'

His mouth twisted. 'Half of them think they own a piece of me.' He looked at her, not teasing any more. 'You didn't.'

Jo's mouth dried. She tore her eyes away from his and stood up abruptly.

'Shouldn't we be getting back? Aren't you supposed to rest your leg?'

He ignored that. 'Are fame and riches really so important, Jo?'

'They make a difference,' she said quickly. 'Of course they do.'

'In what way? How differently would you feel about me if I were poor?'

Her heart fluttered furiously. 'I don't feel anything about you!'

Patrick was not offended. He laughed gently.

'Then it hasn't made any difference, has it? Unless you're saying that you would have felt something if I *hadn't* been rich and famous...' He left it hanging in the air. Not quite a question. More an implication.

Jo set her teeth. Another trap. 'That wasn't what I meant.'

'But it was what you *said*,' he pointed out. 'Very revealing, what people say.'

Her hands clenched into fists at her sides. Her eyes narrowed to slits. 'This is what you do for a living, isn't it? Interrogate people. Tie them up in knots.'

'Have I tied you up in knots, Jo?' There was a smile in his voice.

She shoved her hands hard into her pockets.

'Stop it,' she said angrily. 'Just stop it. I know you think this is funny. But it's not *fair*.'

He squinted up at her. She did not know it, but the sun, filtered through the willow leaves, struck ruby lights from her chestnut hair. She was trembling.

She knew she was trembling. With fury. Jo assured herself that it was fury.

'Why isn't it fair?' It was his furry purry tiger voice. Slow and warm and so damned easy to respond to... Jo felt it slide down her spine like melting treacle.

'You're too good at this,' she wailed.

'This?'

She made a small despairing gesture. 'Please, don't.'

'But it's so much fun,' he murmured provocatively, not moving.

Jo stiffened a spine that was turning to toffee. 'Then it shouldn't be,' she told him honestly. 'I'm no match for you.' And the moment after, she thought: I wish I hadn't said that.

Patrick looked sardonic.

'I'm not,' she insisted, trying to retrieve her mistake. 'I don't know enough. Don't understand enough. Haven't got your education, experience…'

He laughed at her openly.

Jo sought for something that would stop him looking at her like that. 'I haven't got a single GCSE,' she flung at him.

The laughter faltered. A dark eyebrow flicked up. 'Is that an underhand way of reminding me that you're only just out of school?'

Jo looked at him with disgust. 'I've been out of school for years.'

'But you're only nineteen. I'm too old for you, aren't I, Jo?'

Patrick was mocking himself, but there was something about his eyes that made her say swiftly, 'I reckon there are three ages: child, adolescent, grown-up. I am a grown-up. Have been for a long, long time.'

Their eyes locked.

At last, he said evenly, 'You are so sane, aren't you? Sane and practical and kind. You're a rare creature, Jo Almond.'

But he did not touch her. Not even when he stood up and gave an involuntary grimace of pain. Jo made a move as if to give him her arm. But his expression was so forbidding that her hand fell to her side.

He did not say another word as she drove back to the château. When they arrived she swept the car up to the heavily studded main door and turned to him with a grin of triumph.

'Very stylish,' said Patrick. 'You shall drive me again.'

As if he could not help himself, he stretched out his hand and touched her hair.

'A leaf,' he said, tossing it away. 'Jo—will you have dinner with me tonight?'

She hesitated. 'I haven't got the clothes for going out to a restaurant,' she demurred.

'Whose fault is that?' he said, his eyes full of tender laughter. 'But I accept that you wouldn't enjoy it. Here, then.'

Mrs Morrison warned me off, she thought. This must be exactly what she was worried about. Aloud, she said, 'I wouldn't want to upset the Morrisons.'

Patrick was impatient. 'Nor would I. Why should it matter to them?'

Jo snorted. 'I'm an employee. They're employees of much longer standing. Work it out.'

He flung up his hands. 'Okay. Okay. A picnic in the rose garden. Will that solve the problem?'

Jo felt an idiot. 'I suppose so.'

Patrick gave a hoot of sardonic laughter. 'I've had more enthusiastic dates. You are a real education, you know that?'

'Just as well. You can do with some educating about people,' said Jo smartly. She did not like being laughed at like that.

She thought he would snap back. But now that she had accepted him he was positively jolly. 'Add it to your job description. Care of vintage cars and introduction of employer to human sympathy,' he said mischievously. 'I'll increase your salary and then you can afford to buy a stunning dress that I can take you out to dine in.'

Jo eyed him unflatteringly. 'You think you have the answer to everything, don't you?'

'Yup. Pretty much.' He leaned across and,

before she knew what he intended, kissed her cheek lightly. 'See you among the roses. Eight-thirty. Don't be late.'

CHAPTER SEVEN

Nineteen!

Patrick slammed his fist into his bedroom wall.

Of course, Jo Almond was nineteen. He had to remember that.

Oh, she sounded as mature as anyone he knew. More mature than most. She made the ladies' cloakroom coven look like a bunch of giggling schoolgirls. She was cool-headed as a veteran. Resourceful. Strong and brave and—

…and nineteen!

From the first moment he'd seen her, playing like a young otter in the stream, he had known. It was as if she was in a country he could never go back to. She was nineteen and he was thirty-four going on five hundred.

In the car today he had seen the difference between them even more clearly. That guileless honesty! That *skin*…

In his years as a journalist he had seen human

nature at its vilest. Now he reminded himself of some of the details deliberately. You didn't see what he had seen and stay guileless. Oh, he tried to be honest—but it was a long time since he had filed a report that told the simple truth without thinking about the consequences.

What did a world-weary reporter have in common with Jo Almond? Nothing. He never could have.

He knew it. Of course he did. In his heart of hearts. Even though he really didn't want to listen to it. She even worked for him, for heaven's sake. Desire must have driven him momentarily barking.

And then he thought: Not desire. Longing.

And now he had set them up for a romantic meal in the rose garden that was straight out of the Courts of Love. Madness!

'Hands off, Burns,' he said aloud. 'This one's not for you.'

But she did not feel as if she were not for him. She felt as if they were made for each other. As if he had been waiting for her sweet, astringent sanity all his life.

And he heard her crisp voice in his head, *'I reckon there are three ages: child, adolescent, grown-up. I am a grown-up.'*

Oh, you are, Jo. You are.

His body ached with awareness of how grown up she was. And not just his body.

So this is what it's like, thought Patrick Burns, wondering. He was in love, he realised. For the first time in his life.

He planned the evening's picnic with very great care.

First he sent the Morrisons to the cinema with Vincent Petaud from the village. He gave them instructions to stay for a meal after the show and told Vincent not to get them back before midnight. Then he rounded up a long rustic wooden table from the gardener's store, chairs from the kitchen, a starched and rosemary-scented linen tablecloth from a chest that hadn't been opened since the party for Godfrey's funeral, a branched baroque candelabra from the salon.

By the time Jo went shyly down to the rose garden the evening twilight was enhanced by candles, gleaming silver and the scent of a thousand roses stuffed with sunshine. There were even the measured strains of a string quartet.

Patrick, in dark trousers and a pristine white shirt, was frankly stunning.

Jo stood on one leg at the entry to the rose garden. She had sighed with pleasure as she walked through the pleasaunce, where cherry trees were loaded with fruit, marigolds bloomed and birds flitted happily from yew hedge to blossom-strewn ground. But the rose garden offered another dimension to the senses.

'Oh, dear,' she said in a small voice. 'This is a bit out of my league.'

Patrick came towards her with both hands out. 'It's a first for me, too,' he said, taking her hands and leading her to the sundial in the middle of the garden.

'It can't be,' said Jo.

'This? Believe me. Never done anything like it in my life.'

She looked at the goblets and china on the snowy cloth. They reflected the candlelight as if she were looking into another world.

'No one would guess,' she said on a shaken laugh.

'It's distinctly rough round the edges,' Patrick admitted. 'With enough time I would have ordered you troubadours with lutes. As it is, you'll have to make do with Vivaldi on an iPod.'

'It will be a sacrifice,' Jo told him gravely. She remembered troubadours from history and lutes from an old Robin Hood film. 'But I'm sure we'll manage.'

'So am I.'

He raised her hand to his lips. This time she didn't withdraw it.

'This evening,' he said, 'is an exploration. I want to know everything about you. What you like. What you hate. What you want to do with your life.'

Jo put her head on one side. 'Really? And does it work both ways?'

'You'd better believe it.'

'Seriously?'

'Seriously. Ask me anything you want and I'll tell you the truth.'

His mouth stayed serious but his eyes crinkled up at the corners, as if they shared a secret.

Jo shivered voluptuously. It was an exploration, all right. She had never felt anything remotely like this before.

He gave her wine that tasted of peaches and sunlight. It was not champagne but it fizzed gently on the roof of her mouth, making her laugh.

'This tastes nice,' she pronounced.

He looked mildly offended. 'So it should.'

'Well, I never thought I would like alcohol.

Not after my uncle coming home night after night drunk and angry,' she told him frankly.

He nodded gravely. 'Tell me about that.'

Patrick peeled her a tiny, beautiful quail's egg and fed it to her while she told the story. She was matter-of-fact about most of it. Some bits, as she told them now, were even funny. When she described locking Brian in the broom cupboard Patrick laughed aloud.

But when she'd finished he said, 'You seem remarkably forgiving. Don't you want revenge?'

She shrugged. 'Getting away from Carol was revenge enough. She really got a buzz out of putting me down. I suppose I'd like to see they're never allowed to take any other child, though.'

'So would I.' His voice was grim.

Jo was startled. 'Hey, you sound as if you're taking it all personally.'

'I am.'

'Why on earth? If I've got over it—'

'But I'm a nastier person than you, my love,' Patrick told her. 'I still want revenge.'

Jo met his eyes. She saw he meant it. She shook her head, not believing, overwhelmed.

'Hey. Don't look like that. I'm not going on the warpath tonight,' he said softly. 'Drink your wine. It's time we ate.'

Patrick had raided the fridge and the kitchen garden to good effect. As well as the pretty quails' eggs there were tiny spears of succulent asparagus, dripping in warm butter, a crisp salad of lettuce and fresh peas that smelled of the kitchen garden, mighty pâté and sweet roasted peppers, delicate slivers of fish that he told her was trout caught in the river that afternoon, hams and salamis and fat black olives. Whenever he felt she was missing some particularly delicious morsel, he speared it and fed it to her.

By the time the sun finally sank over the horizon Jo was dazzled witless and knew it.

'Will you tell me something?' she said, reaching for some sort of sanity.

'I told you. Anything.' He added reflectively, 'Although I think you already know more about me than most people who've known me all my life.'

Jo was shaken. 'I think it's the same for me,' she said unwarily.

His eyes lifted swiftly at that. She saw them gleam in the candlelight.

'Yes,' he said deliberately.

A solitary bird was trilling. The cicadas scissored busily. A faint breeze, like the river breathing drowsily in the night, lifted the feathers of

Jo's hair from her neck and wafted the evening scent of roses all around them. The perfume was headier than wine: voluptuous damask; tea and nectarine and pepper; cloves and spices. It was hypnotic.

It was magical.

It was dangerous.

She thought: I must go.

But she was rooted to the spot, as if he were a magician and had cast a spell on her.

'Ask what you want,' he said, his eyes intent. She could see little candle flames reflected in them.

'Isabelle—' Jo couldn't remember her full name. 'You said that she wouldn't accept that it wasn't going to happen, you and her. But why did she think it in the first place?'

His eyelids dropped. 'Ah. Yes. Right to the heart of the matter, as usual.' He poured wine into her glass, then sat back and crossed one leg over the other, looking rueful. 'Well, if I have to confess all my sins, so be it.'

She took the wineglass and cradled it protectively against her chest—more for something to hold on to than because she wanted more wine.

'Isabelle managed to convince me—or maybe I convinced myself—that I would have a better chance of adopting Pavli if I were married. I—

considered it. I knew I didn't love her. But I thought it might work.'

Jo flinched. To hide it, she drank in a great gulp.

'Does that shock you, Jo?'

It did, but she was not going to say so. She shrugged, looking away from those mesmerising eyes. 'You told me you weren't a gentleman. I suppose I'm not surprised.'

He gave a quick grimace, as if she had hit him where it hurt. 'Ouch. You don't pull your punches, do you?'

She drank again, too quickly to savour the wine. 'And now? Will you still marry her if that's the only way you can get what you want?'

He stared, utterly silenced. At last he said slowly, 'But surely you know—after what we said today—?'

'You said I could ask anything,' Jo reminded him. Her words came out slightly louder than she'd expected.

'Of course.'

The pale shirt rippled in the almost total darkness as he poured more wine for her. How had her glass emptied so quickly?

'And I'm going to ask the difficult one, too. Tell me about this—Mark.'

She jumped. 'What?'

'The boyfriend who jumped ship. Or maybe didn't.' He sat back in his chair, playing with his wineglass, never taking his eyes off her. Then, as she did not answer, he said incredulously, 'Never tell me that you're still seeing him?'

'Well, yes. But he's not my boyfriend,' began Jo. 'I just ring sometimes to make sure he's all right.'

But her words were slipping every which way, and Patrick was in no mood to listen anyway.

'It's crazy. I know you're ready to forgive everybody almost anything, but this is self-destruct mode. First the guy dumps you. Then you call him to check if he's *all right*.' His mimicry was savage. 'He wants kicking.'

Jo was alarmed. She jumped to her feet. 'You don't understand.'

But suddenly the star-filled sky was doing strange things, and the moon was lurching towards her like a fighter's punching bag. The glass fell from her fingers and spilled the rest of its contents. Jo hardly noticed. She felt very peculiar all of a sudden, and held on to something firm with both hands.

It turned out to be Patrick.

'Ah,' he said, his anger dying as if it had never been. 'The Viognier effect. What's your normal limit, my lovely?'

'Limit?'

'On wine.'

Jo shook her head. Once she started it was not easy to stop, she found.

'I don't have a limit. I've never drunk wine before.'

Patrick gave a laugh that was half a groan. 'Something else I should have asked earlier.'

He stilled her head by the simple means of taking it in both hands.

'You know,' he said conversationally, 'you're absolutely right. I need to learn a lot more about people.'

She leaned against his shirt front. It felt like heaven. She thought he touched her hair. But it could have been her imagination, fuelled by the night, the stars or the wine.

'I'm sorry to say this, Jo, but you're plastered.' He sounded rueful—resigned, even. 'The only thing I can do for you is take you home and tuck you up with a couple of litres of mineral water.'

He must have done just that, though she did not remember any of it. The sun was already high when Jo woke up and her mouth tasted like sawdust. But when she finally struggled upright she saw the bottle of mineral water, half empty, on the bedside table with two of her coffee mugs beside it.

Had he sat with her to make sure she drank it all? Her face flamed at the thought. She felt a total fool. *How* was she going to face him again?

But when she went across to the kitchen for her morning coffee she found she did not need to worry about that any more. He had left for a flight to London before breakfast.

Mrs Morrison, disapproving, said she hoped that meant that he had finished working on his book.

'And telephoning till all hours. He's already at that desk when I go in to open the curtains in the morning. And he's still there long after we've gone to bed. I came down last night to get some hot milk because George couldn't sleep, and I could see the light under the study door. Gone two, that was.'

Jo could just imagine him, sitting at his desk, concentrating, blocking out all thoughts of their evening in the rose garden. Back to his real life, in fact. She felt cold in spite of the morning sun.

George propelled his wheelchair into the kitchen.

'I was looking for you, Jo. Couldn't get an answer earlier. Patrick left you a message.'

Her heart leaped. 'Oh?' she said, trying to keep her tone neutral and forget how her heart raced.

'Yes. He wants you to move all the cars. He's got the Picard brothers coming up to decorate the garage. Doesn't want paint spilled on any of those babies.' And he laughed heartily.

The freeze crept back down Jo's spine. 'Decorating? Yes, of course I'll move them,' she said automatically.

'He said take the day off after that. Go and enjoy yourself.'

She tried. She really tried.

She took a picnic down to the river. But the home-made bread with a sharp local cheese and a few grapes only reminded her of last night's sumptuous fare. And the shimmering ribbon of water and sunshine made her eyes ache as she forgot everything except Patrick Burns.

What had he done to her?

You don't know when you're well off, Jo told herself grimly. Grow up, can't you? You probably won't see him again. He's got more on his mind than you. After last night's little—what did he call it? Exploration. Yes, that's it. Exploration. Like a holiday safari, from which you go back to your real life. He enjoyed it, but now that it's over he's probably even forgotten that you're here.

But when she went back to the barn it did not seem as if he had forgotten.

The main garage had been painted a brilliant white that made her blink. But upstairs—her room was transformed.

Jo ran up the rickety staircase. She just had time to notice that it did not creak, and that the handrail no longer wobbled, before she flung open the door to her domain—and stopped dead.

The walls were now a soft parchment colour. The wooden beams gleamed in the sun. And the furniture—

Looking round, Jo found that now she had a little walnut desk. It was weathered, but it looked like an antique. She touched the pretty thing tentatively, wonderingly. There was also a low table-cum-bookcase that rotated on its own axis, as well as several new shelves on the walls. All were full of books. There was a small scrubbed pine table by the little basin, another by the bed. Everything was old, even the books.

And then she registered the bed. Jo's eyes widened.

It was half as big again as her old iron bedstead. And it was carved and polished and curlicued like something off a film set. It belonged in the château, not the room above the garage. It was a bed for an eighteenth-century beauty with a roguish beauty spot and an abundant bosom. Not for a too-tall half-boy who dressed like a scare-crow even when she bought her first skirt.

Jo snatched her hand from the little desk she was stroking and backed to the door, eyeing the bed as if it was a monster about to pounce and bite.

The pillowcases were edged with lace. The bed had more cushions than the boudoir of a sultan's favourite. What on earth was Patrick Burns thinking of? This was surely not appropriate décor for your standard car mechanic.

Her heart pounded very hard. For a moment Jo stood very still, as if she were afraid. As if someone were watching her.

The thought startled her. She looked round quickly. But, no, she was still alone in the room. Suddenly she did not want to be. She almost fled down the stairs and across to the main house.

Mrs Morrison welcomed her with a beam.

'Pleased with your new stuff?'

'Speechless,' said Jo truthfully.

The housekeeper was pleased. 'Patrick said we were to make you comfortable. Well, as soon as we knew you were a girl I thought the flat was a bit cheerless, too. George looked the stuff out yesterday and the Picards moved it in as soon as they'd finished.'

Jo expelled a long breath. So it was George

who had chosen the flat's new furnishings. She did not have to think of Patrick Burns choosing it every time she put her head on those lace-edged pillows. It was a relief. *Of course* it was a relief. So why did she feel as if someone had just let all the air out of her balloon?

'Thank you,' she said in a muted voice.

She pushed her coffee around the kitchen table. Someone had brought in the post. A postcard in black schoolgirlish handwriting fluttered across the pine. Jo screwed her head round to read it shamelessly.

Patrick, am in France for a couple of weeks. Will call. Love, Lisa.

'Who's Lisa?' she asked with admirable detachment.

Mrs Morrison read the thing quickly. 'Oh, dear,' she said with foreboding.

Jo felt a funny little twist under her breastbone, as if she were jealous of the owner of that black writing. Nonsense, she told herself. Laughable.

George sighed. 'Here we go again.'

Jo was curious. 'Here we go where?'

'Fans, I bet,' said George. 'Patrick won't be

pleased. He calls them bloody silly obsessive groupies. They hound him.'

Jo flinched, as if he were accusing her of doing the same thing. All her fantasies about the curlicued bed with its lavish pillows mocked her.

She banished the thought and fought back. 'Aren't you overreacting? Maybe the woman just wants a cup of coffee and a tour of the house,' she said sharply. 'I bet she doesn't know many people who live in a château.'

Mrs Morrison sighed. 'Let's hope so, dear. But George is right. It's usually these silly girls who see him on television and think they have a chance with him.'

'Oh,' said Jo hollowly.

'In fact, Betty thought he might marry Madame Legrain, just to see them off,' said George, laughing heartily.

Jo felt as if she were drowning suddenly. 'What's wrong with Isabelle Legrain?' she said in a muffled voice. 'I mean, if they're in love….'

'Love? Patrick?' Mrs Morrison was scornful at the very idea.

This was a nightmare. Jo struggled to sound normal. 'Well, maybe she's the one in love and he just wants to settle down.'

Mrs Morrison gave a snort. 'Oh, Madame

Legrain is in love, right enough. With the house. My betting is she'd marry a chimpanzee if it owned the château.'

'He's not lucky in his women, is he?' said Jo painfully. 'Stalked by a college girl or married to a woman who wants his house.'

Mrs Morrison stared.

Jo fled before she finally lost it.

While Patrick was away, the days went slowly. There was not enough work to do on the cars. Jo did a bit of weeding in the kitchen garden for the occasional gardener. But after a couple of days of ferocious activity she ran out of work there, too.

Encouraged by Mrs Morrison, Jo took books to the riverbank. But she could not concentrate on the page. Every time she began to relax she saw Patrick Burns again in her mind's eye; heard his teasing; felt the incomprehensible increase in her pulse. And her whole skin shivered as if she were being caressed by an unseen hand.

'Damn it, it's not *fair*,' yelled Jo, skimming *The Lord of the Rings* across the clearing with the full force of her arm.

She stamped back to the château. 'Can I do anything to help you?' she asked Mrs Morrison, prowling round the kitchen.

'You're feeling ratty,' Mrs Morrison diag-nosed.

'No, I'm not.'

Mrs Morrison raised her eyebrows.

Jo glowered. 'Why should I feel ratty?'

'How should I know? But I've been nanny to too many children not to recognise rattiness when I see it.'

Jo gave a choke of reluctant laughter. 'Oh, all right. I'm a bit—restless.' She stuck a spoon in the great jar of caster sugar on the kitchen table and watched the white crystals cascade back into a pyramid. 'I'm not used to having nothing to do,' she said moodily.

'Oh, is that what it is?'

Jo straightened sharply. 'What else?'

Mrs Morrison did not answer that directly. 'Why don't you go and find yourself a book in the study? Or look at the television? There's a load of videos in there. All the old movies that Mr Godfrey liked. They were here when Mr Patrick inherited. We never cleared them out.'

'Why would I want to sit in the dark and watch videos on a glorious day like this?' said Jo disagreeably.

'Or there's Patrick's tapes of his work,' said Mrs Morrison, unheeding. 'He's been all over the world. You ought to find something to interest you.'

Jo snorted and went to search out some kindergarten weed that had slipped past her that morning.

But that night found her in the study in front of the television, with the curtains closed and carefully labelled tapes spread out all over the rug.

'He does a nice report,' said Mrs Morrison, leaving her with a tray of English tea and some home-made scones.

Jo sat on the rug and pulled her knees to her chin.

Patrick Burns did indeed do a nice report. She took the tapes in order and watched him develop. In the course of one night she saw him age ten years. First jokey stuff in the backwoods, then careful analysis of international diplomacy, then the man of action, keeping up with other men of action, until finally he became the man who saw into the heart of conflict and told the pity of it.

In the last of his dispatches from the cold mountains he was gaunt and driven.

'And the truly terrible thing,' he said, in a voice that seemed to summon her heart out of her breast with pity, 'is that nobody knows how to stop it.'

It was just after that report that he must have been shot, she thought. For the first time she thought, *How?* Had he been trying, in his own way, to stop it? No, that was out of his control, and a clever man like Patrick would know it. But he had been doing something to mitigate the effects of war. Jo knew it in her bones.

He had told her—hadn't he? *'I got them over the border.'* She realised that she was watching him preparing to shoulder his burden and set out. And he had not had a bad leg on the tape. Presumably he had been wounded in his great enterprise.

After the tape finished, Jo sat very still. She felt as if she had walked into a rural railway station and found that it was really a moon launch site. She felt humbled and proud and profoundly moved. Patrick Burns was not just a short-tempered man with a bad leg and a wicked line in teasing, she thought. Patrick Burns was a man who made a difference.

She swallowed painfully. Those tapes had told her more than that Patrick was a man who made a difference to those suffering people in their mountain fastness. He made a difference to her, too. The tapes revealed a new and unwelcome truth.

'Oh, my God,' said Jo slowly. 'I'm in love with him.'

She was shivering as if she was in shock. She

stood up and turned off the video automatically. She felt light-headed and a little sick.

Okay, her blood and her bones and her over-active imagination might have gone out to the man on that tape. But she was still a gargoyle with big feet. A six-foot gargoyle. Just another unimportant detail in Patrick Burns' busy life—as he had already demonstrated. Patrick Burns, who already had more women chasing him than he could bear!

Jo had never felt so unwanted in her life. She turned off the lights, closed up the château behind her and went back to her garage, quiet as a ghost.

All night she tossed and turned in that curli-cued bed. All night, a dream Patrick talked to a camera, not noticing that she was frozen in the snow behind him. Frozen, with her arms out, calling to him.

Just once, at dawn, when the grey light was fin-gering its way along the ceiling beams, she came nearly awake. She knew she had been having nightmares. But for a few seconds she thought she was not alone. She thought Patrick was there in the room. The sensation was so vivid she could have sworn that she caught the elusive scent of his cologne. But when she turned to him murmurously it was only the pillow and the tangled sheets. She was alone. Like always.

'Hell,' said Jo, coming fully awake.

Outside, birds chirped and twittered as the morning turned from grey to silver. She kicked away the tangled sheets and padded to the window. The formal lawns were frosted with brief diamond dew. The shadows of the house and trees had the hard edge of glass. Everything was drenched by a pale, brilliant sunlight. It was utterly still. Utterly beautiful.

And she had to leave it.

I can't stay and become another woman eating her heart out for him, thought Jo, with the sadness of new-found maturity. I must go before he finds out what a fool I am.

There, the decision was made! It felt as if her heart was being torn out by the roots. But it was almost a relief. At least now she knew why she felt so unlike anything she had ever felt before. And, knowing, she knew what she had to do about it.

She went back to bed and pulled the pillow over her head. Her throat felt thick with tears she could not shed. She burrowed determinedly back into sleep. But as she did so, that whiff of cologne, faint as the winds of paradise, touched her again.

* * *

Jo did not tell the Morrisons that she was looking for a new job. But she called Jacques Sauveterre from Patrick's study.

'I thought you had sorted yourself out nicely.' Jacques was puzzled.

'I did. But the job's coming to an end,' said Jo steadily, and nearly truthfully. 'Will you keep your ears open for me? I'll do waitressing—anything.'

He promised. 'And you must come over and see us this week. We have to make some decisions about Mark.'

That sounded ominous. But Jo was too heart-sick to care. She made a date for the only day they didn't go to market, and rang off.

Meanwhile, she flung herself into bringing the cars up to perfection, documenting everything she had done, every supplier she had found, every potential problem she could forecast. Whoever came in to take over from her, Jo vowed, would have the best bloody briefing *ever*.

Gargoyle and scarecrow she might be. Negligible she undoubtedly was in Patrick's life. But she could look after those vintage cars to Oscar-winning standard and he was damned well going to realise it once she had gone.

She was polishing the Bugatti as if her life depended on it when the visitors arrived. She heard someone call out. She turned, startled, pushing back her hair.

There were two of them. They were blond, lithe, gorgeous, and they made Jo feel like an elephant. In contrast to her own light gold dust colour they were deeply tanned. In their cropped tops and brief shorts enough flesh showed to indicate that the tan was probably all over. They looked, thought Jo, young, chic, and very expensive.

'Can I help you?' she said in careful French.

But they were not French. They were English.

'Shouldn't think so,' said the taller one with disdain.

The other was more polite. 'Don't worry. We're on holiday. Isn't this Patrick Burns's place?' she said casually.

She had a voluptuous figure, a swathe of artfully streaked hair and restless eyes. Something about her made the hair on Jo's neck bristle. Years of being homeless and alone had taught Jo to trust the hair on the back of her neck.

But there was no point in denying it. Everyone in Lacombe knew this was Patrick Burns's place.

She said truthfully, 'I suppose so. I don't see much of him.'

The two girls exchanged a complicated look. Complacent, conspiratorial. It said they were not surprised. Jo suddenly realised hotly that her tee shirt was thin and grey with too much washing and her hair was a joke.

But then they shrugged and the look disappeared. They began to chat confidingly. They had walked up from Lacombe, they said. But their glowing energy, to say nothing of their perfect make-up, did not look as if they had just completed a dusty, eight-kilometre walk.

'I'm a great fan,' said the tall one. 'I'll just go up to the château and tell him how much I admire his work.'

Jo was alarmed. The Morrisons had taken George's specially adapted vehicle into Bordeaux. They would not be back until supper time. She was on her own to deal with these uninvited guests.

'He's not here,' she said firmly.

They looked at each other again. This time the look was sceptical.

'That's okay. We'll wait,' said the voluptuous blonde, equally firmly. This time she looked at Jo. Hard.

Jo realised with a little shock that the blonde was not as young as she was dressed. Those eyes were nearer thirty than twenty.

'I'm afraid you can't. He's in London. I don't know when he's expected back. And I'm not allowed to let strangers hang around the cars,' said Jo, inventing hard. 'Insurance—you know,' she added vaguely.

The blonde stared even harder. Under the make-up the pretty mouth was as tight as a rat trap. '*You're* not allowed to? Who are you?'

Jo gave a little shiver, as if she had just met an enemy. Nonsense, she told herself.

'I just help out,' she said, even more vaguely. 'And it's the housekeeper's day off. Now, why don't I drive you back to Lacombe?'

They didn't like it. But when they had been up to the château and seen for themselves the tower of post that was lying on the hall table they accepted that Patrick was not there. Jo, not quite hopping from foot to foot, barred their way into the main body of the château.

So in the end they shrugged and agreed to the offer of a lift.

Jo did not like to take any of the antique cars. Patrick's Mercedes was still in the garage. So she took that. Her passengers, she saw with amusement, were completely unimpressed. She had been right about that, then: they were very expensive, utterly bored by luxury cars. They were interested in the automatic gates, though. And the security system that switched on at sunset.

'I suppose you get electrocuted if you try to climb over?' the voluptuous one said casually.

Jo shrugged. 'I haven't tried.'

'Have you got a key, then? Or don't you go out at night?'

'The dating scene must be rubbish round here,' agreed the tall one with a snigger.

Did that mean she was too much of a gargoyle to date? Jo was outraged. Okay, it was true. But that didn't mean they had the right to say so.

She bared her teeth, and without thinking about it told a lie. 'I date all the time. No problem with getting back. There's a path from the farm over there.' She indicated with a wave. 'It takes you onto the back drive. Those gates are kept locked, too, but there's a stile for walkers.'

That shut them up, at least.

She left them at Lacombe's only hotel. Now they were convinced Patrick was away, what they really wanted to do was leave the village. The English girl even tried to bully Jo into driving them back to Bordeaux, where they had come from that morning. But Jo dug her heels in.

'The Picard brothers run a taxi,' she said. 'The hotel will have their number.'

'That's no use—'

The tall one interrupted. 'It's okay, Lisa. I've still got the number of that limousine place in Bordeaux. I'll call them.'

No doubt that was how they had arrived today, thought Jo. So much for the healthy walk they had claimed. She did not think they had come upon the château by chance at all.

But she did not think they were burglars. They had shown no interest in the beautiful cars or the no less beautiful antique table in the château. No, their motive was transparent: Patrick. For all their pretty tans and designer labels, they were as predatory as sharks. Maybe George hadn't overreacted to that groupie's postcard after all.

I'll have to tell Patrick, she thought worriedly. As long as I see him before I go.

But when she got back to the château she found that seeing him again was not in doubt. He was on his way back from the airport.

CHAPTER EIGHT

JO BOLTED for the garage. Yes, she would tell Patrick. But—not yet. She needed to get her head together before she saw him.

She left Mrs Morrison excitedly baking a coffee and walnut cake for someone called Simon Hatfield, whom he was bringing with him. Mrs Morrison had known Simon ever since he and Patrick had been at university together, and she couldn't wait to cook for him again.

On the whole, Jo was glad that someone else was coming to stay in the château. It would be easier to avoid Patrick if he had a friend to distract him.

She'd miscalculated. She was just outside the garage, polishing the Rolls-Royce as if her life depended on it, when she heard a quick, brisk step on the gravel behind her.

'Hi,' said Patrick, as if he had never been away, as if he had not disappeared from her life without so much as a goodbye. 'Missed me?'

Jo whipped round. He was standing with his hands on his hips, laughing. She could not help it. Her heart leaped to see him. She found she was smiling back. More than smiling; beaming like an idiot.

His eyes were so warm she hardly recognised him. 'How was the hangover?' he said softly.

'An experience. It was my first. Hangover, I mean. I am,' said Jo, dazzled by the warmth in his eyes, 'having a lot of firsts these days.'

'Sorry I couldn't be here to help you through it. Did you drink the rest of the water I left you?'

He must have sat on the edge of her bed and put the mug to her lips...

Jo put down her chamois leather very carefully. 'Yes. Thank you. Very thoughtful. I wouldn't have known what to do.'

'Sometimes you're a quaint old-fashioned thing,' mused Patrick. 'There can't be many nineteen-year-olds who haven't learned how to treat a hangover.'

He wandered round the Roller and into the garage. He was, she saw, hardly limping at all. He sniffed the air.

Jo pattered after him. 'New paint,' she explained.

'I know.'

'I didn't know you were going to have it

painted. And—the amazing new furniture. Thank you.'

His turned, his eyes caressing. 'I wanted to give you something. That was all I could think of on the spur of the moment.'

It would have been nicer if he'd chosen it himself, Jo thought perversely. 'Thank you,' she said again.

'There are clothes, of course,' he said, adding mischievously, 'But I think they'd better wait until I can come too, don't you?'

Her eyes flashed. 'I am perfectly capable of choosing my own clothes.'

'But I will have so much more fun out of it.' He wandered round the Bugatti. 'Do you like the rotating book table? I've had that in mind for you for some time.'

'*You* chose my new stuff?' Jo could not believe her ears. Surely Mrs Morrison had said that George had looked everything out for the garage apartment?

'Left Nanny Morrison a list,' he said blithely. 'Down to the books from the library. How many have you read?'

And the lace-edged pillows? thought Jo involuntarily. She blushed and looked away. *But he chose the furniture himself.*

'None yet. I'll get down to it tonight.' Inside, she was almost dancing with delight. *He chose it himself.*

He looked disappointed. 'I hoped you'd have dinner with Simon and me. I want you to meet Simon. You'll like him. And he certainly approves of you.'

She was bewildered. 'Approves of me? He doesn't know me.'

'No, but he knows your advice. He thinks it's sound. And so are you.'

'I don't understand.'

His eyes danced wickedly. 'Come to dinner and all shall be revealed.'

She was not proof against that naughty look. 'Yes.'

But it was not to be. Almost at once his mobile phone rang.

He looked at the caller's number and snapped it open. 'Sorry.'

He listened for some time, his expression slowly darkening.

'Why is it that you clever lawyers can pull out the stops for a silly harassment charge but can't deliver on something really important?' he asked his interlocutor acidly.

Jo felt sorry for the person on the other end of the line.

Patrick listened for another, longer space of time. 'That is really inconvenient,' he said grimly. 'But if he's flying out tomorrow I suppose there's no choice. Okay. We'll be there.' He cut the call.

Jo said it for him. 'Dinner's off?'

'Postponed,' Patrick corrected swiftly. He touched her cheek briefly, as if he could not help himself. 'I think you'll be pleased when you know why, though.' He looked at his watch. 'Damn! I'll have to go and prise Simon away from his love fest with Nanny Morrison's cooking. See you tomorrow, sweetheart.'

He did not wait for a reply. It was just as well. Jo was dumbstruck.

Sweetheart!

Too-tall scarecrows with shoulders like a wardrobe didn't get called sweetheart. But she did. She had. She hugged it to herself all through the day. After supper she could not concentrate on any of Patrick's books because the word went round and round in her head. She could not stop smiling.

It was a breathless night. The heat of the day had not been dispelled when the sun fell. Instead it seemed to stay around, baking the ground, making the stones of the garage sweat, keeping the air as still as an assassin waiting for his victim. And, of course, there was Patrick's 'sweetheart' to keep her restless.

In the end, Jo gave up on sleep. She slipped out into the garden and walked down to the fountain.

It was there that she heard a sound. A sound she should not have been hearing. Hardly believing what was in her mind, Jo went soft-footed towards it. She peered round a trim box hedge and her heart sank.

They were back, all right. They were not even bothering to keep their voices down. She could make out their dark figures distinctly, strolling up the back drive. And *she* had told them how to get in, Jo thought in dawning horror.

She turned and pelted for the château.

It was in darkness, but when she tried the back door was unlocked. The kitchen was empty. So, a cursory glance showed her, was the drawing room and the study. But she could make out a light in the conservatory. She ran down the corridor and pushed open the heavy glass door.

She was still out of breath. 'Patrick,' she said urgently.

He was reclining on a bamboo sofa, going through some papers in the light of a small table lamp. He stood up when she came in, his brows looking concerned.

'What is it?'

Jo blinked. He was wearing jeans and a short-sleeved white shirt. She had never seen him dressed so informally before. It made him look bigger, somehow, and powerfully attractive. The jeans flattered his long length. The shirt contrasted with his tan and threw into relief the muscles and sinews of arms, neck and shoulders.

And this was the man she was in love with? She was crazy. She didn't stand a chance!

Her breathlessness was no longer due entirely to running. 'Patrick,' she said again, on a wavering note. 'I should have told you when you came to garage the car but I forgot. I'm so sorry. I've done something awful.'

He looked at her with an unfathomable expression for a moment. Then his mouth tilted quizzically.

'How awful?' he asked.

Jo drew a deep breath and launched into full confession. 'There were some girls here earlier. I took them back into Lacombe but... They asked me and... I told them how to get in by the back drive. I didn't *think*. I'm so sorry.'

She waited for one of his famous explosions. It did not come.

'I see,' he said at last. 'And from your dishevelled state, I take it you've just bumped into them on the premises?'

'Well, they're only in the garden so far,' Jo said fair-mindedly. 'But I'm pretty sure they won't stay there.'

'So am I,' agreed Patrick dryly. His eyes crinkled. 'Stop hovering. You look like a neurotic stork. Sit down and let us think about this.'

Jo sat on the very edge of a wicker chair. It was completely surrounded by trails of weeping fig, so that the brightly striped cushions almost looked as if they were placed directly on the vegetation. It was quite the most uncomfortable seat she had ever had in her life. She fixed her eyes on him anxiously.

Patrick's look was full of lazy appreciation. 'Very Amazonian. All you need is a machete.'

Jo looked down. She was wearing her sleeping shorts, and all of her scuffed, tanned legs showed. She blushed. Fortunately, Patrick was already turning away, reaching for a telephone behind a tub of lilies that looked as if they had tongues and teeth. Jo decided that she didn't like exotic plants.

'Simon?' Patrick was saying into the phone. 'You weren't asleep, so stop moaning. Can you join me? I'm in the conservatory.' There must have been objections from the other end because he said, 'Yes I know. Never mind that now. Something's come up. Rather a nuisance.' He paused longer this time, to listen to the other's reasoning. 'Well, switch it through to here. Press the back slash and then dial—' he looked at his phone '—twenty-eight. Soon as you can, please.' He broke the connection and turned back to Jo. 'Don't look so worried,' he said softly.

'But I've been so stupid. I've let you down.'

'No, you haven't.' His tone was gentle. 'You were a little unwary, perhaps. It happens to all of us sometimes.'

Jo felt guiltier than ever. 'Don't be kind to me, Patrick.'

His eyes were pure gold in the soft light of the reading lamp. He looked at her for a moment without speaking, holding her gaze so that she could not look away.

'Why not?' he said softly.

Jo could not answer. Her eyes widened wonderingly. The silence between them lengthened. A leaf fell from a plant somewhere and the dry little sound made her jump. But still Patrick sat looking at her with that mesmerising half-smile. Jo's heart began to race.

But then a dapper, balding man with bright eyes and rumpled hair bustled in. Simon Hatfield, Jo deduced, swinging round on her seat.

'I hope your blasted extension system works. They said they'd ring me back tonight,' Simon Hatfield said.

Patrick stood up and went to a small bamboo cupboard that Jo had not noticed before. 'Drink?'

'Thought you'd never ask. Whisky, please.'

'Jo?'

She shook her head. 'I've had enough hang-overs for this week,' she said ruefully.

Patrick laughed aloud. 'Grapefruit juice, then.'

Simon's eyebrows rose. Patrick introduced them swiftly and brought the drinks back to the bamboo table. Jo put his papers on the floor to make room for the glasses.

'You,' Simon told him, 'are a horrible slave-driver. If it weren't for the fact that I'm going to charge you a fortune for this, I'd tell you to call the office.'

But he sat down and sipped his drink with a friendly smile.

Patrick grinned. It was clear that they were friends. 'You're a fraud. You would kill for a week of Nanny Morrison's cakes.'

'You may have point,' Simon agreed. 'So, what's this nuisance?'

Patrick's grin died. 'Possible trespass.'

Simon looked at Jo. His bright eyes were full of speculative interest. She blushed and tried to tuck her long, bare legs out of sight under the chair.

'No, not Jo,' Patrick said with a quick frown. 'She works here. She saw the forces of darkness advancing. I want you to get rid of them for me.'

'I draw the line at murder,' Simon said peacefully. 'At least while I'm notionally on holiday. If you want to prosecute for trespass get a French lawyer. I haven't a clue what to do.'

'Then think about it,' Patrick advised. 'I've had enough of being pursued by media groupies.'

Simon looked weary. 'Oh, another assault of the "My Night With the Stars" brigade?'

'I imagine so.'

'Well, we've seen them off before.'

'And last time,' said Patrick dryly, 'it cost me my job and a lot of friends. Can we think about damage limitation this time?'

'Sure.' Simon's smile was bland. 'Just point

out there's a lady in residence,' he said, with a wave in Jo's direction. 'Trophy's already won. They go away. Easy. That's my considered professional advice.'

Patrick looked at Simon for inscrutable minutes. Jo thought that if she were Simon she would be shifting from foot to foot in growing discomfort. But the lawyer maintained his cheerful affability.

'That's your best shot?' Patrick asked at last.

He did not look at Jo at all.

'That's *your* best shot,' Simon corrected. 'Nothing to do with me if you're a lust object for every woman under ninety. I'm just telling you what makes sense. From my vantage point as an informed bystander.'

Patrick's brows twitched together in a line of black displeasure. He said curtly, 'You don't know what you're talking about.'

Simon flicked at glance at Jo. 'What's your opinion—er—Jo? What would discourage you most if you'd managed to chase Patrick into his lair?'

Jo shook her head. 'I can't imagine it,' she said with fervour.

For some reason that made Patrick frown even more blackly.

'Jo's my employee. I'm not tangling her up in

my private disasters,' he said sharply. 'And I don't need any advice that tells me otherwise.'

'Fine,' said Simon, showing signs of annoyance at last. 'Then I'll deal with the little matter of family support and you deal with this tinpot crisis in your own way.'

They glared at each other for a fraught minute.

Then Patrick gave a soft laugh. He shrugged quickly.

'You're right. I'm getting it out of proportion. Put it down to frustration.'

Simon's eyes rested briefly on Jo. 'Oh, I do.'

Patrick said hastily, 'Another Scotch?'

Jo said, 'Family support?'

Simon looked thoughtful. 'I gather it was your idea? Patrick withdrew his application to adopt and offered to buy up some bombed-out buildings to house the whole group. In theory foreigners can't own property. But we've worked out a wheeze whereby the people own it collectively. He will support them and arrange rebuilding. It's a great solution.'

Patrick was pouring drinks when Simon's telephone rang. Simon flicked it open, spoke briefly, and listened for longer. Once he pulled a pen and leather-bound notebook from the breast pocket of his jacket and made a careful note.

When he put the phone down he looked at Patrick soberly.

'Congratulations. You own a village street.'

Jo stared.

Patrick was absolutely still. Eventually he said, 'And that means?'

'It means they stay together. Pavli gets to live with the Borec family. You can send in builders whenever you like. The Red Cross are happy to let their local man live there, too. They won't monitor formally, but he'll be around. So the warlords will think twice about trying to muscle in.'

Patrick said nothing. He was very pale.

Simon said in a slightly injured voice, 'That's the best I can do. I think it's a damned good settlement. Much more than I expected, to be honest. That guy at the airport this evening must have been really impressed.'

Patrick let out a great whoop. He scooped Jo up from the sofa and swung her round. 'Simon, you're a marvel. Jo, you're a genius. Now we're cooking with gas. When can we get started?'

Simon broke into a grin. 'Want to go and sign the agreement now? I can fax from the library, can't I?'

They went, still talking hard.

Jo got up and began to move restlessly along the overhung pathways of the conservatory.

The low reading lamp cast odd shadows, making the tall conservatory seem even taller and the hanging foliage somehow dark and vaguely menacing. In the silence after the men's departure Jo became aware of the sound of water trickling. She traced it to a stone cherub on the far wall, out of whose mouth a desultory trickle of water played on a series of stone bowls beneath. She looked at the water lilies in the lowest bowl.

He had listened to her. More, he had followed her advice. *Her* advice. No one had ever done that. He'd said she was a genius. Patrick Burns, who made a difference to the world, had said she was a genius.

She realised she was trembling.

I'm not just in love, she thought. I think I've just committed my whole life.

It was exhilarating, but also a little frightening. She sat very quietly in her dark corner of the conservatory and let herself recognise that she was committed to Patrick Burns.

Great swathes of headily scented, leathery leaved stephanotis twined round the pillar beside the artificial pools. They effectively hid from sight anyone standing by the little fountain. Unless, of course, you already knew there was someone in the conservatory and came looking for them.

The girls who slid open the window at the end of the conservatory clearly did not know. They were talking in excited undervoices.

'Lisa, are you sure…?'

'Shut up and give me a hand.'

There was the creak of windows being opened. One of the girls scrambled through and gave a shriek as she impaled herself on a spiky-leaved plant. At once there was silence.

What do I do now? thought Jo.

While she was still debating, the girl, reassured by the lack of reaction, had found a safer place for her feet and let herself down with a thump.

The big glass door opened hastily.

'Jo?' said Patrick, from the doorway. 'Are you all right?'

Jo had her mouth open to answer, to warn him, when there was a small rush and the table lamp was extinguished. Patrick said her name again. And then there was a breathless little laugh, a patter of lightly soled feet and Patrick saying furiously, '*Jo*—what the hell—?'

Jo did not need to use her imagination very much to know why his words were so sharply broken off. It was quite obvious from the murmurous little noises that Lisa was making.

Oh, *Lord*, thought Jo. And he must have thought it was her, flinging herself at him in the darkness. She felt hot at the thought. Blundering, she started forward. She found the tumbled table lamp without difficulty. She righted it, her brain working rapidly. Immediate action was necessary. Another lady in residence, Simon Hatfield had said. Could she do it? What would Patrick say if she did? He might not, thought Jo, shivering a little, thank her for it. But Simon had said it would work. And Patrick wanted damage limitation.

Lisa was saying, 'Hi, gorgeous. You took a rain check at the office party, remember? And now I'm here to deliver. Oh, Patrick, Patrick...'

Patrick said, in a voice like an ice cap, 'Lisa from Reception. What did I do to deserve this?'

Jo made her decision.

She knew what to do. She knew how it had to look to be convincing. Just think of Jacques and Anne Marie, she told herself. And keep a seat belt on your heart!

Quickly, Jo ran her fingers through her soft locks, mussing them into what she hoped would look like the disorder of a disturbed embrace. She hauled her old tee shirt out of her shorts and pushed it so that it fell off one shoulder. She kicked off her soft shoes.

Then she turned on the light and went towards them, yawning artistically. She looked—or she hoped she looked—like a girl ready and waiting to make enthusiastic love with her lover. In her imagined scenario Patrick was returning to continue where he'd left off. All she had to do was make it plain to Lisa that there was no room in his life for anyone else.

They were both staring at her. Lisa had her arms tight round Patrick's neck. He was straining away from her embrace. In the shock of the sudden light her arms fell reluctantly. Patrick looked frustrated—and furious. When he saw Jo, his mouth fell open.

Jo felt a flutter of nervousness in her stomach. She quelled it. She was taking Simon Hatfield's professional advice, she reminded herself. She contrived another yawn and her eyes met Patrick's.

'I'm sorry, darling. I didn't hear you come in. I fell asleep,' she said, hoping it sounded intimate enough.

He said nothing. Well, at least he hadn't repudiated her yet, Jo thought, trying to look on the bright side.

She looked at Lisa and gave her a cheerful grin—the sort of grin that the lady in possession would be likely to give an intruder who offered no contest. At least, she hoped so.

'Hi. Back again?'

Lisa was looking stunned. She was very pretty, Jo noted—not for the first time.

'Yes. I wanted— I mean, I thought—'

The girl's eyes slid up to Patrick's austere profile.

Jo stepped up to Patrick, slipped her hand into the crook of his arm and leaned her head against his shoulder. It was unyielding. She hoped it did not look as harshly unwelcoming as it felt.

Experimentally, Jo turned her face against the material of his shirt, like a stroked cat. It made Patrick's shoulder muscles stiffen, but he did not protest.

The scent of the shirt and his body under it was disturbingly familiar. Swallowing, Jo tried to repress the little shivers of excitement which were threatening to destroy her concentration.

From her vantage point against his shirt Jo smiled at the girl, who had stepped awkwardly away. 'Did you leave something behind?'

Patrick drew a deep breath. Jo felt his chest rise under her cheek.

'You said you didn't come into the house,' the girl said accusingly.

Patrick seemed to make a decision. He put his arm round Jo's waist.

She could not help herself. She gave an involuntary shiver, as if he had touched a nerve. Something deep inside her fluttered into vibrating life.

Patrick said, quite gently, 'I can't see that our private arrangements can be of interest to you, Lisa.' He took Jo's hand and held it against his heart, looking down at her tenderly.

Jo's breath almost stopped in her throat. Oh, when he played a part, he played it wholeheartedly, she thought, startled. Never mind Lisa, he almost had Jo believing that it was love looking at her out of those amber eyes, inviting her to drown herself in emotion.

It might even be true. Only—how could she tell? The man was sex on a stick; beautiful girls climbed into strange houses to get at him. He looked at Jo with more affection than anyone else she had ever known. He hugged her. He kissed her hand. But he was a demonstrative man. He hugged Nanny Morrison, too.

Oh, how did you know what a man like that was feeling?

She managed a tremulous sigh. It was not entirely play-acting.

Lisa looked from one face to the other. Her mouth tightened. Suddenly, she did not look so pretty any more. She said hoarsely, 'You're lying.'

But it was clear that she had doubts, at least.

'There was nothing about it in the papers. They said you'd come back from the war zone, injured. They never mentioned *her*.'

'So now you know something the papers don't. Congratulations.' Patrick was suddenly crisp. 'Now, it's time to go. Where's your friend?'

Lisa went silently to the window. Feeling as if manacles had been struck off her, Jo straightened. But Patrick did not let go her hand. To her astonishment, she felt his hold tighten. She looked at him, bewildered.

The other girl's head appeared in the window.

'I heard,' she said miserably. She sounded as chastened as Lisa did not. 'We shouldn't have come.'

'No, you shouldn't. A taxi will take you to wherever you're staying.' Patrick turned back to Lisa. 'And if you ever—*ever*—invade my home again, I will tell Mercury and you'll get your cards. Do you understand?'

She tossed her hair. '*You're* the one Mercury sacked. Not me.'

'You're out of date,' said Patrick curtly.

Lisa gaped. 'Everyone said Lassells would never forgive you. And that you'd never forgive him.'

'They were wrong.'

Over her head Patrick met Jo's eyes. Amazingly, she could have sworn there was amusement there. Shared secret laughter! How sexy it was!

'Lassells knows a good thing when he sees it. I am. And he wants to do a programme on my book about the escape, too. As for me and my temperament—that's all over.' He was talking to Jo, not Lisa. His eyes danced. 'I'm going to have a family to support.'

Lisa looked over her shoulder and saw Jo's face. That was what convinced her in the end.

They left, subdued.

Patrick saw them off at the kitchen door. Making sure they got into the Picards' taxi, as he told Jo. Throughout, he held on to her hand absentmindedly. As the car lights disappeared down the drive she tried to withdraw it and failed. He looked at her, his mouth curling in mockery.

'I suppose you think I ought to thank you for coming to the rescue?' he said dryly.

He still did not let go her hand. She felt a flush rise under those searching eyes. She was not under any illusion that he was grateful.

'I couldn't think of what else to do,' Jo muttered.

'You could, of course, have done nothing.'

Which he would no doubt have preferred.

She bit her lip. 'I'm sorry. I meant well.'

Patrick gave a soft laugh. 'You know the one about the path to hell?'

'I—'

'I've never believed in clichés. I'm beginning to think I was wrong.'

Jo was so surprised that she stopped tugging at her hand.

'What?'

'Here we are, doing absolutely everything from the best possible motives, and God knows where it's leading us,' he said. The strange eyes searched her face. 'Or do you know, Jo? I sometimes wonder how much you do know behind that funny little face of yours. Where do you think this is all going to end?'

She swallowed. *How can you tell what a man like Patrick Burns means?*

He sighed. Then, freezing her into immobility, he lifted their clasped hands, turned them round, and touched her soft palm to his mouth. He held it there. Jo felt his lips against the sensitive hollow: gentle as a feather, indelible as a brand. She shivered.

End? Where was it going to end? She didn't even know what had started, she thought. She stood there, looking down at the dark head, her long legs trembling uncontrollably.

'Please,' she said. It was barely audible.

Patrick looked up quickly. His face changed.

He said her name on a swift breath.

Jo's eyes fell. She was aware of a nervousness she had never felt before. It was amazingly strong. She had learned any number of tricks in the last few years to control or at least disguise trepidation in difficult circumstances. Now they all seem to have deserted her.

It bewildered her. She was not afraid of him. She was not afraid of anyone these days. She had learned to take care of herself in far worse circumstances than this. Patrick was a man she trusted, a man she respected; a man, moreover, who had been kind to her. And she was deeply in love with him. She couldn't be afraid of him. Could she?

The fluttering in her wrists felt like fear,

though. So did the cramping constriction on her breathing. Yet if it was not fear of Patrick Burns, then of what?

He said her name again. Reluctantly, Jo lifted her gaze. The yellow eyes were compelling. And oddly hesitant. She searched his face. She seemed to be drawing closer to him of her own accord, in spite of the wild trembling of her legs.

She did not know whether he reached for her or whether it was she who closed the gap between them. All she knew was that she melted into his arms. He kissed her softly, his mouth gentle on her eyelids, her lips, her throat. It was slow and infinitely controlled. It set off little earthquakes along the pathways of her nervous system. She moaned. Patrick feathered his tongue round her lips. The earthquake was not so little this time. Jo squeezed her eyes tight and shivered at the feelings bubbling within her.

'Oh, sweetheart. Are you sure?' Patrick murmured against her mouth.

She could feel him preparing to put her away from him. Outraged, hungry, frantic not to waste all that brave courage, she wound her arm round his neck and held on.

'I'm not a child, Patrick,' she said to him furiously. 'Don't treat me like one.'

She pressed herself against him. And suddenly he was not in control any more.

Jo clung to him hard. Her legs were shaking violently. She recognised that she was scared. But she knew that this was what she wanted. Had wanted since that day by the stream, if she were honest.

Patrick said her name in a startled voice, as if the intensity of her response shocked him. So he couldn't know how she felt about him. Jo recognised dimly that this might be a problem in the future. Very dimly. She had other things on her mind at the moment.

His hands tightened. Jo moulded herself to him. She thought her spine would crack with the pressure. She did not care.

His mouth left hers and travelled the sensitive skin of her throat. Jo could feel the hammer thuds of his heart under the restricting clothes. The hands that held her were not completely steady.

'This is too soon. It's madness,' he muttered hoarsely.

But he said it against the warmth of her naked shoulder. And he did not let her go.

The disgraceful tee shirt slipped, caught, was bunched up in seeking hands and ripped. They both heard it.

'I don't believe I just did that,' groaned Patrick. 'What a cliché.'

Jo laughed breathlessly. The night air was like a warm feather stroking across her flesh. It was not the night air which set her shivering, though.

She caught his hand and held it under hers.

'Come back with me,' she said huskily.

He lifted his head then. She could feel him scanning her face in the darkness.

'You said I would be undisturbed in the flat unless I asked you back,' she reminded him.

In spite of the shivering she laughed again, a soft sound of pleasure and self-knowledge and trust. Above all, trust. She moved under his hand. Patrick caught his breath.

'I'm asking,' Jo whispered.

He swept her up against him, so fiercely that she imagined she could feel the blood running through every vein and artery in his body. She kissed his mouth feverishly, then his forehead, his cheekbones, the unshaven jaw, the muscular column of his throat.

'Please,' she said, between little kisses.

Patrick groaned. 'Jo, you don't know…'

But she put her hand over his mouth and kissed his ear, trembling and laughing at the same time.

'Please.'

He shook his head. But he did not let her go.

'I must be mad. We both must be mad,' he said, but his arm was round her strongly and he was urging her towards the barn.

Jo tried to unlock the door. Her hand was shaking so much she could hardly get the key in the lock. Patrick took it away from her and twisted the key with an impatient flick of the wrist. Inside, he turned to her and pulled her into his arms again.

They made their way up the staircase, kissing and touching, murmuring to each other. Although there was no need, neither of them raised their voice above a whisper.

Jo did not even try with the lock to her flat. Patrick unlocked it one-handed, without lifting his mouth from hers or detaching a long arm from round her waist. As soon as the lock gave he swung her up into his arms and shouldered his way into the room. Jo gave a choke of startled laughter and clung on for dear life.

He kicked the door shut behind them.

'Very stylish,' she murmured. 'I take it your leg is better?'

Patrick glinted a look down at her in the darkness. 'Doing the physiotherapist's exercises every day. More of your good influence.'

She laughed softly in her throat. Is that me sounding so sexy? she thought. She was half startled, half gleeful.

'I'm impressed,' she purred, practising her new-found skill.

'Good.'

He carried her across to the bed and dropped her on it. Then he bent and switched on the bedside light. Jo lay among the lace-edged pillows, her tee shirt disgracefully ragged and no covering at all. She laughed up at him, stretching tanned arms above her head. She had never felt so alive in her life.

His eyes were pure amber. As he looked down at her his mouth was severe, but his eyes danced.

'Very stylish.' He used her own words to tease her, stroking the chestnut fronds that lay against the tender curve of her neck. 'I'm impressed.'

Jo looked up at him for a long moment. The laugh died out of her eyes. Slowly she reached for him, her expression serious.

'You will be,' she vowed.

At her urging he came down to her. Jo's fingers went to undo the buttons of his shirt, but he caught and trapped them between his own. He looked at her soberly.

'My darling.' It was so soft she hardly heard it.

He pushed her hair back with an infinitely gentle gesture that somehow made her want to cry. He swallowed. 'You're so young. Are you sure?'

Her smile twisted. 'Not that young,' she said, trying to keep it light.

It was too late to keep her exit route clear, she thought. Not that she wanted to any more. But she had to keep it open for Patrick. He must not know how desperately she was in love with him. Her fingers twitched in his at the thought.

He looked down, startled by the movement. Then, as he had done before, he raised their clasped fingers to his lips.

'You say that now, but…'

She leaned across and stopped the words on his mouth.

'I'm sure,' she whispered.

This time he did not stop her when she fumbled the buttons open.

If she had thought about it, she would have expected Patrick to take charge of their love-making at once. But he did not. He lay back, his hands behind his head, his smile tender, and let her undress him.

At first hesitant, soon Jo was exploring his body in wonder. She had never imagined such closeness, such trust. When she saw the terrible scars on his leg, her eyes filled with tears. She touched her fingertips to the place gently, then brushed her cheek and her hair back and forth across the puckered skin, trying to take the re-membered pain away with her touch.

'Oh, that tender heart,' said Patrick.

Jo looked up. He was teasing her gently, but she thought she caught the echo of pain in his words.

'Don't feel sorry for me, Jo,' he told her quietly.

She shook her head, denying it. But she was too choked to speak. He reached a hand down and tucked the soft chestnut hair behind her ear.

'You're so beautiful,' he said, almost to himself.

And in that moment she felt beautiful.

He began to kiss her then. At first it was slow, almost playful. But soon the play turned serious, and they were gasping with a need which Jo, in-experienced as she was, realised was mutual. Patrick did not make love to her as if she were too young to know about passion or too light-weight to mean it. He made love to her as if she was all he ever wanted.

There was just one moment of hesitation when she recoiled involuntarily. It did not hurt, but it was such an indescribably new sensation that she caught her breath.

At once Patrick checked. But Jo clung to him fiercely. She was beyond thinking, beyond control. She was all fire and feeling.

'I love you,' she said.

CHAPTER NINE

SHE said it again, more than once through the whole of that hot, short night. Every time she did, Patrick silenced her with a passionate response that took her higher and higher, to the stars and beyond. But he never said that he loved her.

It was very early morning when Jo awoke. She knew it was early because the air was still cool, although the blaze of light in the window across from her bed was pure gold. She stirred, giving a sigh of perfect contentment. She could never remember feeling this peaceful, this *happy*, before.

She turned her head on the now hopelessly creased pillows. Patrick was asleep, face down, one arm possessively flung across her body. His face was turned towards her so that she could see the long sweep of eyelashes and the beautiful, haughty line of cheekbone and jaw.

Jo smiled. He did not look haughty now. He looked as if a great weight had been lifted off him; as peaceful as she felt, in fact. He was smiling in his sleep. She touched a gentle finger to the corner of his mouth in wonder.

She felt him wake under her touch. He frowned, muttered a little, the long lashes flickered. Then one golden eye opened and met her enquiring gaze. For a long moment he absorbed her. Then his smile widened.

'Good morning,' he said softly.

Jo realised suddenly that she had been holding her breath. She had not been quite sure how Patrick would react to finding her beside him in the morning. She gave him a brilliant smile in her relief.

'Good morning.' She kissed him, and then said mischievously, 'Did you sleep well?'

Patrick gave a mock groan and turned onto his back, pulling her down onto his chest. He ruffled her hair.

'Eventually. What about you?'

Jo's smile was blissful. 'Best night of my life.'

Patrick chuckled. 'First of many.'

He swung his legs out of bed and trailed off to her shower, unself-consciously naked. Jo listened to the rush of the newly installed power shower and lay back against the pillows, hands behind her head. It felt so right. Home, she thought. Blissful.

He came back with a towel wrapped somewhat insecurely round his slim hips.

'You shower. I'll make coffee.'

When she emerged, he was standing at the small gas ring, on which her coffee maker was bubbling cheerily, and leafing through *The Furry Purry Tiger*. The towel had already slipped dangerously.

He looked up from the book. 'Poor Jo,' he said with compunction. 'If this were a proper seduction we would be having champagne and fresh croissants.' He spooned granules into her thick mugs.

Jo went across to him and dropped her head against one warm, bare shoulder. She sniffed.

'Sorry. I've never seduced anyone before.'

Patrick put an arm round her and rubbed the top of her arm companionably. 'No, but I have. I should have done better. I will next time.' His eyes were warm, but he looked at her searchingly. 'No regrets?'

She shook her head vigorously. 'No regrets.'

He kissed her. 'Long may it stay that way.'

Something in his tone made her lift her head to look up at him.

'You don't sound very confident,' she teased.

'I'm not,' he said soberly. Then, seeing her hurt expression, he went on quickly, 'Mine is a wicked world. There are a lot of people out there who won't want to leave us alone. It won't be long before they invade this dream time of ours.'

Jo shook her head. 'You're imagining it. No one out there is the least bit interested in us.'

He looked unconvinced.

'And even if they were,' she said blithely, 'we're not interested in them, so it doesn't matter what they say.'

But she was wrong. And it was not Patrick's world that invaded their dream. It was hers.

She was having coffee with the Morrisons as usual when the phone call came.

'Do we have to tell them?' she had said to Patrick, uneasy.

He was shrewd. 'That we spent the night together? Don't you want to?'

She shook her head, suddenly shy.

'I thought you said you didn't want to tell any more lies?' he teased. But his eyes were shadowed for the first time that morning.

'I don't, but—I don't feel comfortable with this,' she said.

He touched her face. 'Always so honest.' He sounded sad. 'Okay. Have it your way. I won't say anything if you don't.'

So she was sitting having coffee, listening to the big news about Simon's arrangements for

Patrick to take care of his refugees, as if she had not heard it all at the time, when George answered the phone and said, 'It's for you, Jo.'

'Me?' At first she thought it had to be Patrick, calling from somewhere to tell her to get to his side at once; he couldn't live another hour without her. But then she answered.

'Jo? Jo—they're here. They say they're going to take me back.' It was Mark.

He was nearly incoherent with panic. But Jo managed to calm him down enough to get the salient facts.

Jacques, impressed by Carol all those years ago, had called the Greys.

'I should have known,' said Jo, white to the lips. He had been so evasive on the telephone. She had even been uneasy at the time. She just hadn't bothered to question him. Too busy thinking about Patrick, of course! 'I should have known.' It was a cry of anguish.

'Jo, they're going to take me back with them. Carol says they can prosecute, and they will if I don't go with them. Jacques says they're my legal guardians. Brian isn't saying anything, but he isn't drunk so Jacques thinks he's okay. Jacques just says I have to go. But Anne Marie told me to call you.'

Thank God for Anne Marie.

'I'm coming now,' said Jo.

She turned to George. 'Where's Patrick?'

'He went to Lacombe.'

Her shoulders sagged. 'So he's taken the Mercedes?'

'No, he walked.'

Her head came up. 'Then I need the keys. Now.'

The Morrisons tried to stop her.

Wait for Patrick, they said. At least call him on his mobile, they said. But Jo was too distraught. All she would say was that it was all her fault and she had to go *now*. All they could do was press a small bag of Mrs Morrison's scones into her hand, along with a couple of bottles of water.

As soon as she'd gone they phoned Patrick.

'Jo's gone. It's someone called Mark,' said George.

Patrick swore, long and hard.

Mrs Morrison took the telephone from her husband. 'Don't listen to him. He doesn't know what he's talking about. Jo was hardly making sense, poor lass.'

'If she wanted me, she'd have called me.'

'You didn't see her. She was really shocked. Crying and trying not to let it show, and frantic with it.'

'I'll kill him,' said Patrick.

Mrs Morrison didn't answer that. 'I reckon something really bad has happened. I think you ought to get after her. She needs you, Patrick.'

Patrick thought. 'Okay. Here's what you do. Find out what number called her this morning. Call it back. Don't mention Jo, act stupid, but find out the address. That's a starting point.'

'George can do that,' said Mrs Morrison. 'Acting stupid comes naturally to him. Oh, and she took the car.'

It was a nightmare drive through the winding lanes. Once she backed herself up a farm track and had to go right into the farmyard before she could turn round. She put on the brakes and drummed her hands on the wheel in frustration. That was when she realised her face was wet with crying.

Jo took hold of herself.

'This has to stop. You'll never convince Jacques that Carol is a manipulative harpy if you go in gibbering. Deep breaths, Jo. Deep breaths. Mark depends on you.'

She made herself take a long draught of mineral water. She even managed a mouthful or two of scone and felt immediately better. Then she switched on the engine again and let the Mercedes coast gently back to the winding lane. She didn't lose her way again.

The smallholding was deserted when she arrived. There was a shiny red car outside, with the label of a well-known car hire firm on the windscreen. The Greys', presumably.

When Jo went into the little farmhouse that had been so welcoming it was a shambles. No one about, but plenty of evidence of some major activity—maybe even a fight. A chair had fallen backwards and just been left to lie. There were papers all over the scrubbed wooden table. And it looked as if someone had picked up a soft sports bag and flung it at the wall. Its contents were scattered over every bit of furniture in the place. It looked violent.

'Oh, Lord. Brian!' said Jo, alarmed.

She pelted out into the field behind the house, scanning the landscape. The goats were gone, too, she noticed, though probably that didn't mean anything. There was nobody on the horizon. She could not think of what to do next.

And then, toiling up the lane, she saw Anne Marie. She rushed to meet her.

'What's happened? Where are they? Is Mark all right?'

'I need some water. Let's go inside.' Anne Marie put a hand to her side.

Suddenly Jo had a wholly new source of alarm. 'Are you all right?'

Anne Marie tried to laugh, but it broke in the middle. 'I have a stitch. I am not about to give birth. Let's get out of the sun and I'll tell you everything.'

Carol and Brian had arrived, bringing a lawyer and some impressive-sounding threats, at mid-morning. Jacques had started off being reasonable, but Anne Marie had seen that Mark was terrified.

'That is not like Mark,' she said, pouring her second glass of water.

'No,' agreed Jo. Tears pricked her eyes. She dashed them away with the back of her hand.

'So I told him to go into the office and telephone you quickly before any decisions were taken. Only, being Mark, he did more than that.'

Jo looked up. 'He ran away?'

Anne Marie blotted her forehead. 'Put sugar in the hire car petrol tank, we think. Let the goats out. While Jacques was chasing them, *then* he ran away.'

'Sugar! I wouldn't have thought of that.'

Anne Marie shrugged. 'When he didn't come back the Greys started to go after him. They couldn't get their car to start. Brian said it was sugar. Now we are waiting for the hire company's mechanic to come.'

'The Greys have gone after him on foot?'

Anne Marie shook her head. 'Their lawyer gave them a lift to town. They will be back. With an order that says Mark is a delinquent and has to be restrained, I think.'

She began to cry.

'This is awful,' said Jo. 'Worse than I thought. What on earth can I do?'

But at that point she didn't have to do anything. The door to the lane banged back and Carol Grey stormed in. She had scratches on her arms, twiggy bits in her hair and one of the straps of her smart high-heeled sandals was broken. When she saw Jo, she stopped dead and hissed, like a bad-tempered cobra.

'*You,*' she said with loathing. 'I might have known you'd be at the bottom of this. You great moronic lump.'

And from the shadowy entrance to the garden a cool voice said quietly, 'Mrs Carol Grey, I presume?'

Jo yelped and swung round on her seat, staring into the shadows as if she could not believe it.

Patrick Burns strolled into the room.

'How long have you been there?' gasped Jo.

He was not looking at her. 'Jo told me what a thoroughly unpleasant person you are,' he remarked, in a light, social voice.

That voice would, thought Jo, have frozen her to the marrow if she were Carol.

'You know, I thought she was exaggerating? I was wrong. She didn't tell me the half of it.'

Carol bared her teeth at him. 'And who might *you* be?'

'Call me a friend of the dispossessed young,' Patrick said.

Carol did not understand that. But it sounded impressive, and even vaguely official. Jo saw her hesitate, look at Patrick with half recognition.

She said, 'I'm Mark Seldon's legal guardian. I know my rights.'

'Somehow I doubt both those statements. Now, *I* think,' said Patrick, sitting down opposite her and giving her the sweetest possible smile, 'that you are a bully who manages to convince people that you know better than they do.'

Oh, he was clever, thought Jo. Even if he had overheard her discussion with Anne Marie, he could only have half the facts. Yet he had summed up Carol Grey in a heartbeat.

'I think you enter into unlawful contracts to care for children the authorities don't know about. In fact, I'd be surprised if Jo's mother ever knew what happened to her daughter.'

Jo's head reared up. What was he talking about?

Carol said, 'You're crazy.' But she sounded scared.

'Who was it, Mrs Grey? Who put Jo into your so-called care? Not her mother. I'd put good money on it.'

'She was a student. Her parents did the right thing for the unwanted brat,' blustered Carol. But her eyes shifted from side to side and the viperish antagonism had gone out of her.

'Oh, I don't think anyone would believe that—including those controlling grandparents. Not if they knew how you'd mistreated the children in your care.' He flicked through the papers on the table with evident disdain. 'I think that if the authorities knew what you'd done, you would probably be prosecuted. Certainly you would not be allowed to foster any more children—even privately.'

Carol stared at him, her painted lips working. No sound came out.

'*I* think,' said Patrick charmingly, 'that it's time the authorities knew. And I'm the man to tell them.' He did look at Jo then. His face was quite expressionless. 'With the evidence of Mark's ill treatment and Jo's sworn statement.'

Carol made a sound that was hardly human, somewhere between a groan and a roar, and jumped for Jo.

Patrick moved so fast Jo hardly saw him. He flung the big kitchen table aside as if it were made of paper and got Carol into a solid arm lock.

'That will help, too,' he said.

Carol began to scream abuse.

By the time Brian and Jacques returned she had calmed down somewhat. She also knew she was beaten.

'No point in sticking around here,' she said sullenly to her exhausted husband. 'Stupid little cow has got big money on her side. Call for a cab and let's go.'

Jacques looked truly appalled. It had never occurred to him that pleasant, sensible Mrs Grey could be such a monster, he said.

'Appearances can be deceptive,' said Patrick. He was looking at Jo now, but his eyes were still empty. 'You can think you know everything there is to know about someone, but you've only seen one side of them. Dodgy things, people. Trusting them is dangerous.'

That's for me, thought Jo. *He's saying he trusted me and I didn't trust him back. And he's right.*

Her face twisted with regret. But she could not say anything in front of the Sauveterres. It was too personal. Too painful. Even if it meant that she never told him how sorry she was, she could not do it here.

Patrick made himself at home in the simple kitchen. The Sauveterres thought he was wonderful. So, too, did Mark when he came back at last, and Patrick congratulated him on his enterprise. So did the well-tipped car hire mechanic when he came to tow away the Greys' devastated machine.

Only Jo sat there, silent and out of the general buzz, lost in her own miserable thoughts. She had had a night of total happiness. And then she had destroyed everything by her own silly, impulsive actions.

At last Patrick moved. 'Time we were going,' he said to Jo, pleasantly.

She stood up. 'You mean—you want me to drive the Mercedes back to the château?'

He frowned. 'You haven't been listening at all, have you? No, I will send someone for it tomorrow. You and I are going back in the Bugatti.'

She stared. 'You mean—you still want me to come back with you?'

His mouth twisted. 'Of course.'

'But—I didn't trust you.'

He looked right at her then. Into her. His eyes wide and golden and utterly naked.

'But I trusted you,' he said simply. 'Now, let's go home.'

CHAPTER TEN

As IF in a dream, Jo went out to the car with him. She hugged Anne Marie and Mark. She did not look at Jacques. He'd meant well, but he was too conventional to see the truth of things. He was not Patrick.

The open-topped Bugatti was the favourite of her charges. Or maybe her former charges. She said cautiously, 'Have I still got a job?'

Patrick started the stately car, waving like some old-world maharajah as they pulled away from the smallholding. 'If you want one.'

'I do,' said Jo fervently.

'Good.'

He knew the roads better than she did. He did not lose his way once.

Eventually, Jo summoned up her courage and said, 'I'm sorry I didn't tell you about Mark.'

'So am I.'

So he hadn't forgiven her. Her shoulders

slumped. 'I know I should have. But I was never sure—'

'That I'd keep your secret?' he finished for her savagely. 'You don't have much faith in me, do you, Jo?'

'I had faith in Jacques Sauveterre,' she flashed. 'You see where that got us.'

'I,' said Patrick between his teeth, 'am not Jacques.'

Her momentary temper dissipated. 'I know. I know. I'm sorry. I should have trusted you.'

'You certainly should have. Do you know that I've had horrible sleepless nights worrying about that bloody boyfriend of yours?' he said furiously. 'If I'd known it was your foster brother you were concerned about, I wouldn't have worried.'

'You were jealous?' said Jo, fascinated at the thought.

'I thought you were deranged,' Patrick corrected coldly. 'An emotional masochist. Worrying about a guy who'd dumped you at the first opportunity.'

Jo didn't believe him. 'You were jealous,' she said with satisfaction.

He relented. 'All right, I was jealous. A first for me. I don't like it. Don't let it happen again.'

'Again?'

'From now on,' said Patrick firmly, 'you're mine. Got that?'

Jo opened her mouth on an indignant retort, met his eyes and closed it again, stunned. It could not be Patrick looking at her with such fierce protectiveness. It could not.

She swallowed and looked down at her brown fingers.

'Seriously?' she said in a small voice.

'Seriously.'

He smiled across at her. The tenderness was still there. And something else.

'Where do you want to go, my lady? Paris? Venice? The mountains of the moon?'

She did not recognise him in this mood. 'Wherever you want to go, I suppose,' she said helplessly.

'You'll leave it to me?' His smile grew. 'Excellent. Then we shall go to my favourite place.'

They drove sedately through a small town, drowsing in the afternoon sun, watched only by a couple of wide-eyed children. Patrick waved to them graciously.

They went at a gentle pace along back roads. The Bugatti was higher off the road than the modern car, and Jo could see farther over the quiet countryside than she was used to. In spite of this change of perspective she was almost certain that they were going back to the château. She looked sideways at Patrick and decided not to ask.

Instead she said gravely, 'Patrick, what did you mean when you said that to Carol about my mother?'

'Ah.' He slid the car into a small passing place and stopped the engine. 'I'm sorry about that. I should have told you first. But it was only a suspicion until she confirmed it.'

Jo was bewildered. 'Have you been digging up stuff about my birth parents?' She was angry. 'I told you I didn't want—'

Patrick took both her hands and held them strongly. 'No, my love. No. Of course I wouldn't do anything like that.'

'But you must have been spying on me?'

'Well—in a way—'

'That's despicable,' Jo interrupted hotly. 'Snooping through my past—'

'Jo, listen. It has nothing to do with your past. I looked at your children's book.'

She was utterly confounded. 'What?'

He gave her hands a little shake. '*The Furry Purry Tiger*. Remember? I was looking at it this morning. You said it was all that you had of your own except your birth certificate and your passport. Well, I read it this morning.'

'So?'

'Jo, I know about books. It was never properly published. The only snooping I did was on the Internet, to check with the second-hand book traders. Their back catalogue confirms it. *The Furry Purry Tiger* is all yours. Your mother wrote it for you. Probably illustrated it and had it privately printed for you.'

Jo's eyes widened and widened. 'How can you tell?'

His eyes were tender. 'Does it matter? It's the truth. Do you still not want to find her?'

She swallowed. 'I'll have to think about it,' she said in a small voice. 'Can we drive on now, please?'

He scanned her face worriedly. But when she motioned him to start the car again, he did.

'I wouldn't really have spied on you,' he told the road.

She didn't answer.

He gave a despairing laugh. 'Jo, please talk to me. I don't know where I am here. Is this about my being so much older than you?'

She snorted.

'I'll take that as a no,' said Patrick, sounding a

little happier. 'Because I was your employer when last night happened, then? Because you were still in my power to some extent and I should have been more—restrained?'

'Not a gentleman,' muttered Jo.

'Yes, okay. Not a gentleman, if you like. You *can't* have thought I'd sack you if you didn't come across? Can you?'

She said nothing.

'Did you feel...' he hesitated, sounding sick '...harassed?'

'I didn't feel in the least harassed,' Jo said furiously. 'What sort of wimp do you think I am, Patrick Burns? Did it seem to you that last night I felt harassed? Did it?'

His mouth tilted. 'Not at the time,' he admitted. 'I had some bad moments when you ran away this morning, though.'

Jo swung round on her seat and inspected his expression, to see if this was some obscure mockery. But his face was perfectly serious.

'I didn't run away,' she protested. 'I was trying to protect my own.'

'I know. But, you see, I thought after last night *I* was your own, too. Why didn't I get a share of the action?'

'You did,' said Jo. She dwelled pleasurably on

the thought of Carol's face when she'd realised that Patrick had bested her. 'It was wonderful.'

He sent her a sideways look. 'Not unwarranted interference? Not spying on you?'

'No.' Jo swung round in the seat and beamed at him. 'Not spying at all.'

'Well, thank God for that.' He sounded as if he meant it. 'So, don't let me find out about your next disaster from the Morrisons. We're on the same side, remember? From now on your battles are my battles. And vice versa.'

It sounded like heaven. Suddenly, the road was blurring in front of her eyes. She sniffed and rubbed her nose hard.

She found a crisp laundered handkerchief being pushed into her grubby paw as the car slowed.

'You are the love of my life,' Patrick said softly.

Jo mopped at the corners of her eyes. 'I'm sorry for being difficult. I've been on my own for so long, you see. And I was responsible for Mark being here in France. I know I—' She stopped as the enormity of his words sunk in. 'What did you say?'

The car coasted silently to a stop beside a gleaming hedgerow. Meticulously, Patrick applied the handbrake and switched off the engine before turning to face her, one arm along the back of her seat. His eyes were dancing.

'You are the love of my life,' he repeated obligingly. 'Everyone else knows it. Simon. The Morrisons. Even that damned interfering physiotherapist. It's extremely irritating to have them all tell me to do what I've been trying to do for days.'

Jo ignored the last part of his remark. Her eyes widened and widened.

'Love of—but you—I—you said—I *can't* be,' she stammered.

He took her hands between both of his.

'Jo. Listen, my darling. I said a lot of damn silly things. You don't seem to see it, but I'm not a nice man, you know. I'm cold and arrogant and I don't give a stuff for the majority of my fellow humans. I wouldn't take responsibility for Crispin the way you cared for Mark for a million bucks.'

She had seen the driven, reckless fury in him. 'I know,' Jo said softly.

He looked surprised. 'Do you? Maybe you do. You know an awful lot in your way, don't you, Jo?' He pulled her into his arms. He did not kiss her, but rubbed his face against her soft hair over and over again.

'After I was shot I seemed to be completely powerless. I'd lost my job. I couldn't adopt Pavli. Couldn't make anything right that we in the West had done so wrong. I felt that I was a total waste of space in a vile world. And then, that day by the stream...' his voice softened '...I saw you.'

Jo blushed. She drew herself out of his arms and smoothed back her disarranged hair.

'I remember.'

His eyes gleamed. 'I'm glad of that. You looked so—happy. Just playing around in the water. And then you saw that kingfisher and you looked—enchanted. I wanted that. I wanted to feel like that. And I wanted you.' He paused expectantly.

Jo blushed harder and held her peace.

'As I think you knew,' Patrick said, amused.

She swallowed. 'I—er—I didn't realise. I wasn't very experienced in things like that.'

'No? So why did you run away from me that day?'

Jo stared at him in some dudgeon. 'I said I wasn't experienced. I didn't say I was a fool. I knew there was something going on—and it was out of my league. Of course I ran.' She drew a deep breath. 'I'd been on my own for years. I'd been through some sticky moments. I never really had too much trouble with sex, though. I was too busy surviving. But I knew it had to be handled carefully. And that it was best left alone by people like me.'

Patrick looked amused and concerned at the same time.

'Why people like you?'

'People,' Jo explained carefully, 'with no one to run to if things go wrong.'

He winced. 'I was afraid of that. That's why I was so torn about telling you how I felt. You had nowhere to go if you didn't feel the same.'

Jo stared at him. 'But I did feel the same. I do.'

The hand on her face stilled. 'So why didn't you come to me for help this morning?' said Patrick, as if he couldn't get this failure of trust out of his mind.

'I wanted you. You weren't there. Then I had to do something, fast, and...I wasn't absolutely sure that it would matter to you,' Jo said simply. 'I mean—you'd never said you loved me or anything...'

Her voice trailed off into silence at his expression.

'What did you say?' Patrick said in a frozen voice.

Jo lifted her chin. 'Don't start bullying me. It's

true. We made love all night and you never said you loved me. Not once. And I,' she said with sudden rancour, 'did.'

'Oh, my darling,' said Patrick remorsefully. 'You're right. What an idiot I've been. I should have thought. Told you.'

'Yes, you should,' Jo said crisply.

She was beginning to feel a great happiness building up inside her head. But she was not going to admit it yet. 'You knew I didn't have experience in that area. You should have realised I'd need a clear message.'

Patrick smiled straight into her eyes. It was a heady sensation. The happiness was very close to overflowing.

'Then I'll tell you now,' he said. 'You are the love of my life. I don't want to live any longer without you beside me. I won't marry any other woman if you won't have me. I am not good enough for you. But if you'll marry me I'll do my best to care for you and love you and not disturb the kingfishers for the rest of our lives. How's that?'

'Message received, loud and clear,' said Jo softly. 'Yes, please. I'd love to marry you.'

The happiness spilled over. Laughing, she leaned forward and kissed him. He held her as if she were very precious. They kissed for a long time. Then he put her away from him, smoothed the hair out of her eyes with a hand that was not entirely steady, and turned back to the steering wheel.

'Where are we going?' asked Jo, suspiciously.

'I've told you. My favourite place.' Patrick sent her a mischievous look as he started the car. 'Nice and private, with a beautiful view.'

Jo began to laugh.

He went on solemnly, 'I'd like another chance to see that kingfisher. And you might like to swim again. I'll even join you this time.'

And so he did. Eventually.

EPILOGUE

A YEAR later there was a small ceremony at the château.

The restored gardens were opened to the public, to support a refugee village in a distant mountain range. The cheerful crowd also paid large sums to be driven round the grounds in one of Patrick Burns's famous vintage cars. Mrs Burns drove the Bugatti.

Among the crowds was Mrs Burns's brother, a budding racing driver by his own account. Also a tall woman with chestnut hair, whose relationship to Mrs Burns was unmistakable. Not just because of her elegant height, either. It was the way she could not take her eyes off her laughing daughter.

And at the end of the day dashing Patrick Burns strode up to the podium and switched on the microphone. After a welcome, and some words about the village they were supporting, he waved a hand to the turrets behind him, just touched with the first rays of midsummer.

'When my wife first saw this place it was tired. It had seen too much and was falling apart at the seams,' he said. 'Rather like me.'

Much laughter in the crowd.

Tim from Mercury Television said under his breath, 'God, he's good.'

'But she loved it,' said Patrick Burns. 'She said it should have pennants flying. So—'

There was a fanfare. From the turret of the Ladies' Tower a thin flag unfurled and fluttered bravely in the breeze.

Patrick stood back and raised his arm. Across the crowd his eyes met Jo's. The love, the laughter, the total trust were there for all to see.

'My lady's standard,' he said.

MILLS & BOON® PUBLISH EIGHT LARGE PRINT TITLES A MONTH. THESE ARE THE EIGHT TITLES FOR SEPTEMBER 2006

---❦---

THE GREEK'S CHOSEN WIFE
Lynne Graham

JACK RIORDAN'S BABY
Anne Mather

THE SHEIKH'S DISOBEDIENT BRIDE
Jane Porter

WIFE AGAINST HER WILL
Sara Craven

THE CATTLE BARON'S BRIDE
Margaret Way

THE CINDERELLA FACTOR
Sophie Weston

CLAIMING HIS FAMILY
Barbara Hannay

WIFE AND MOTHER WANTED
Nicola Marsh

MILLS & BOON®

Live the emotion

0806 Rc

MILLS & BOON® PUBLISH EIGHT LARGE PRINT TITLES A MONTH. THESE ARE THE EIGHT TITLES FOR OCTOBER 2006

PRINCE OF THE DESERT
Penny Jordan

FOR PLEASURE...OR MARRIAGE?
Julia James

THE ITALIAN'S PRICE
Diana Hamilton

THE JET-SET SEDUCTION
Sandra Field

HER OUTBACK PROTECTOR
Margaret Way

THE SHEIKH'S SECRET
Barbara McMahon

A WOMAN WORTH LOVING
Jackie Braun

HER READY-MADE FAMILY
Jessica Hart

MILLS & BOON®

Live the emotion

0906 Rom LP